FENDER

KINGS OF RETRIBUTION MC LOUISIANA

CRYSTAL DANIELS

SANDY ALVAREZ

TWO PENS -
CRYSTAL *Daniels*
Sandy ALVAREZ
-ONE STORY

1

FENDER

My thoughts are all over the place as I sit at the back of the bar, enjoying my glass of bourbon. The powerful aromatic of oak from the barrel the liquor was aged in permeates my senses before the rim ever touches my lips. I have a love-hate relationship with the bottle. It's both my enemy and savior. For that reason alone, I shouldn't drink tonight. I don't claim to be perfect. I'm flawed in many ways, and right now, I just want one drink and to play music. Hints of caramel, vanilla, and spice coat my tongue and warm my throat. Life is heavy these days. My mom is fighting cancer, and I'm sitting here wanting to drown my worries in whiskey. I'm a card-holding momma's boy. Not ashamed of it, either. While I'm sitting here feeling the burn of alcohol, purposely putting something into my body that is no good for me, my sweet mother is sitting at home handling the effects of chemo. I close my eyes and savor the flavor of the bourbon while convincing myself not to have another.

A beautiful brunette walks by, and I look twice because she bears a close resemblance to a girl I once knew. Her eyes lock with mine, and I realize aside from the color of her hair, she looks nothing like the girl I loved.

My thoughts drift back in time. I think of her more than I care to admit. I loved her.

I stare at the glass in my hand.

Love can kiss my ass.

"You alright, brother?" Wick asks, and I can hear the concern in his tone as he takes a seat at my table.

I tilt my head back, not wasting a drop, and the last bit of whiskey has a delicious burn as it slides down my throat. I set my glass down on the bar. My brothers know nothing about my first love. All they know is the fact I've been burned by cupid's arrow and have zero interest in getting reshot by one. However, the club is aware of my mom's health, and they all know the stress I've been under from coping with it. "I'm good." My answer is short and my voice is tight. He eyes me, knowing damn well I'm a liar. The truth is, I'm stressed.

I catch sight of Tequila making her way toward us. She stops at Wick's side, and his arm snakes around her, his hand coming to rest on her pregnant belly. Tequila leans down and kisses her man. Her eyes settle on me. "Hey, Fender."

"How you doin', gorgeous?"

"Aside from needing to piss every five minutes, and having a massive craving for cornbread and a glass of milk, I'm fine." She sits in the empty seat. Her eyes soften. "How's your momma doing today?" The weight of their stares makes me uneasy.

I let out a heavy sigh, then stand. "She's the same."

"She's a strong woman, brother. She'll beat it again," Wick says.

Not this time. I keep my thoughts to myself. Instead, I nod. "I'm about to take the stage. Any requests?" I plaster on a smile.

"Play whatever's in your soul, brother," Wick states, and I walk off toward the corner of the bar where the modest stage is located. I pick up my guitar and drag the stool close to the mic and take a seat. I strum the strings a few times, making sure they're in tune. It's Saturday night, and Twisted Throttle is packed. It's the perfect setup for someone looking to get lost themselves.

My mouth hovers close to the microphone. "How's everyone doin' tonight?" My voice resonates throughout the bar. The patrons shout and yell, with a few females who scream out my name.

"Take me home," a beautiful woman with sandy blonde hair shouts, and I zero in on her. She's sitting with a group of female friends. Her eyes sweep over me seductively, undressing me with her imagination. I give her my best panty-dropping grin, then strum the first chords to Joe Cocker's "You Can Leave Your Hat On."

After the first song, I move into Creedence Clearwater Revival's "Bad Moon Rising," where I feel myself relaxing deeper into the music. This is when the crowd's noise slowly fades, and all I hear is the sound of my guitar. I take a brief pause and grab the bottle of cold water I sat on the floor near the base of the mic stand before taking the stage. I down half the bottle then start belting out "The Ballad of Curtis Loew," and the barroom slowly becomes nothing more than a room full of hushed whispers as I sing.

I'm not anywhere I thought I would be in life, but exactly where I belong. Years ago, I dreamt of sold-out crowds and fame. I wanted to see my name in the marquee lights. I was going places —going to hear my voice on the radio someday. Then I met Riggs and Wick. They gave me a regular gig here at Twisted Throttle. Over time I got a glimpse of MC life and what the brotherhood had to offer. It appealed to me more than chasing my name in lights ever did. Almost a year later, after landing my regular gig at the bar, I was paying my dues prospecting for the Kings of Retribution. Now, here I am, Sergeant at Arms.

Just as I'm finishing the song, I catch a commotion near the front of the bar, where the tables sit at the opened windows. A biker who strolled in with his traveling companions earlier keeps putting his hands on a young lady who's attempted to walk by his table a couple of times after trips to the bar. She spins, spilling the drink in her hand down the front of the asshole's cut. The biker laughs and his buddies join in. It doesn't sit right with me. I lean into the mic. "Hey, asshole." Many sets of eyes turn toward the stage, but I narrow in when he looks at me. I point at him. "Yeah, you. Keep your hands to yourself, motherfucker."

"Only having a bit of fun, brother," he shouts, then turns to his biker buddies and shares a laugh.

I set my guitar down in its case. "I'm not your brother. Touch her again, and you're out of here," I warn. The biker's face turns red and twists with anger. I've pissed him off by calling the bastard out in front of the entire bar, but I don't give a fuck. I don't claim to be the good guy in any story, but one of many things I don't tolerate is putting uninvited hands on a woman.

I exit the stage and walk across the room to where my brothers are sitting with their women. Everest is standing off to the right, his focus across the room on the group of bikers. "Keep an eye on that bunch," I tell him.

"Already on it, brother." Everest nods and heads for the front door to be closer to the bikers.

"Anyone notice their patch?" I spin a chair backward and straddle the seat.

"Want another drink?' Keri asks as I look up at her.

"I'll take water, sweetheart. Thanks."

Keri smiles, then heads around the back of the bar, returning promptly with my cold beverage of choice.

"Their cuts say Reaper's Nomads." Riggs lifts a beer to his lips and takes a drink. "They're just that—nomads. A bunch of bikers with no roots. Like gypsies, they live life on the road traveling from one place to another."

"So, you've heard of them?" I swipe a cigarette from the pack sitting in the center of the table, along with the matchbook sitting beside it. I strike the match and light my smoke, then inhale deeply until my lungs burn. "What kind of reputation do they have?" I ask on an exhale.

Luna signs to Riggs, telling him she's done for the night and will wait for him. Riggs leans into his woman and kisses her on the neck. What he signs to her, I won't say, but it makes Luna turn several shades of red. He swats her ass as she walks away. "The kind that looks for trouble," Riggs finally answers me.

Not two seconds after Riggs says these fuckers are trouble, we hear a commotion and look across the room at Everest getting jumped by five of the sons of a bitches. Wick turns to Tequila and orders, "Upstairs. Now."

The packed bar soon starts to empty as patrons file out the door onto the street to avoid getting caught up in the brawl. I rush toward the fight along with my brothers, each clashing with a biker, evening the playing field.

I go straight for the motherfucker I called out moments ago. He sees me coming and smirks. The asshole swings first, his fist clipping my shoulder after I sidestep to avoid the blow. I'm quick to throw a punch of my own, clocking the ugly fucker against the side of his head, causing him to stumble back against the table where he was seated. Beer bottles roll off the table and shatter on the floor. He rushes at me, taking another wild, uncontrolled swing and missing. I land another blow to the bastard's head, putting him on his knees. To the left of me, Kiwi cracks a barstool across the back of another biker. Over by the front door, Riggs is beating the face of another. I look down at the worthless pussy at my feet just in time for him to come up swinging a broken bottle with jagged edges. I lift my foot and bury the bottom of my boot in his face. He falls back against the tabletop behind him. I hover over him, blood already gushing from his broken misshapen nose, and snatch his sorry ass up by the collar of his cut. I notice his name patch: Red, Vice President. Then I proceed to beat him, grinding my knuckles against his face repeatedly until he no longer moves.

Out of the corner of my eye, I see Nova approaching. "He's done, brother." His words cause me to pause, and I look down at my knuckles, coated in the biker's blood. The bastard is out cold. Before releasing my grip on him, I rip his name patch off his vest, then walk away. The urge to have another drink hovers, like the devil whispering in my ear as the adrenaline rush subsides. I glance around the bar, looking at what the mayhem left behind. A couple of broken tables, along with a few stools, lie in pieces on the floor. Shattered glass lies in puddles of beer and whiskey too. "You alright?" Nova tosses me a bar rag to clean my hand, then proceeds to do the same, wiping blood from his knuckles.

"I'm good." I search the room, counting heads and assessing the current state of the rest of my club members. Kiwi is sporting a cut over his right eye. Everest has blood splatter on his cut, but by the looks of it doesn't belong to him. I watch Wick close the entrance door and draw the shades over the windows, keeping outsiders from looking in. Riggs pulls his gun from beneath his cut, pointing at one of the battered bikers as Wick and Everest toss the other men, placing them together.

"On your knees, motherfuckers." Riggs growls the order, and the ones who can still stand lower to the floor alongside the one Riggs' barrel is aimed at. I stride across the room, coming together with my brothers, standing behind our President. The biker in Riggs' crosshairs happens to be this MC's President; his name is Butch. His bottom lip is split open, with what appears to be a tooth protruding through his raw, bloodied flesh. The fucker spits at the floor, his crimson saliva hitting Riggs' boot.

"You'll pay for this," Butch sneers in defiance.

"Wrong, motherfucker." Riggs uses his gun to clock the son of a bitch across the face. "You and your men better get the fuck out of my city, tonight. You're lucky we're allowing your sorry asses to walk out of here breathin'."

Butch laughs manically. "I don't know. I've taken a liking to the Crescent City." He smirks. "Perhaps we might stay awhile."

I react to the sudden movement of one of the bikers reaching into the waistband of his pants by drawing my weapon. I press the cold end of the metal barrel right into his busted eye socket. "Move another muscle, and I put a bullet through the back of your skull."

Nova leans down, searches the bastard, removes a black mini revolver from his waist, then steps back, unloads the barrel, and pockets the bullets and weapon.

Riggs speaks again. "Anyone else stupid enough to try another stunt like that?" He pauses a beat, never taking his hardened stare off the Nomads President. "If you value the lives of your men and the breath in your lungs instead of your club's cold bodies in unmarked graves, I highly recommend you rethink your intentions and ride out of town. In fact, I suggest you leave Louisiana entirely. One of you shows your face around here again, we kill you. Now get you and your trash out of my bar."

The beaten bikers get to their feet. The one I fought can barely stand on his own, and his buddies have to help walk him out of the door. Bourbon Street is still bustling with party-goers with plenty of good times to be had. Music continues keeping the atmosphere lively as if nothing ever happened. A few onlookers watch on as we escort the Reaper's Nomads to where they left their rides, with our weapons tucked from view to not draw any more unwanted attention.

The sound of horse hooves hitting the asphalt snags our attention as our unwanted guests mount their bikes. Officer Jenkins, who we call Hollywood, tugs the horse's reins to stop. He eyeballs Riggs. "There a problem?"

Riggs walks up and offers a handshake. "Nothin' we can't

handle, Hollywood. Just helping our friends here and wishin' them safe travels."

Hollywood glances at the situation, nods, then looks at Riggs. "How's my bike coming along?" He ignores the obvious fact we've beaten the fuck out of these men and instead asks about the custom bike the shop is working on for him.

"It should be ready by the end of the week," Riggs says casually.

"I'll see you then." Hollywood gives one final look back at the Nomads, then back at us Kings. "You men have a good night." He then takes his leave.

Nothing more is said as the Nomads start their bikes and slowly ride away. Riggs eyes Everest and Wick. "Follow them." The two nod and walk away. Riggs turns to face Kiwi, Nova and me, and sighs. "Let's get shit cleaned up." We follow him back toward the bar.

"I have a feelin' this isn't the last we'll hear from Butch and his men," I state.

"I have a feelin' you're right, brother," Riggs agrees.

2

JO

"Ladybug, let's get a move on!" I shout, stepping out onto the front porch. "Come on! We were supposed to be on the road an hour ago!" I prop the heavy box in my arms onto my hip while slinging my purse over my shoulder. The scorching Tennessee sun beats down on top of me as I load the last of my belongings into the back of the U-Haul. Blowing out a frustrated breath, with the back of my hand I wipe away the beads of sweat running down my forehead and peer back over my shoulder in search of my daughter, who has been M.I.A. all morning.

"I spotted her out back in the treehouse earlier," Aunt Maggie says as she makes her way down the gravel driveway toward my car.

I let out a heavy sigh.

"She's just upset. This move is a big change for her," my aunt assures.

"I know. It's a big change for me, too. It would be easier if she wasn't hell-bent on digging her heels in about it."

Two months ago, I was laid off from my job. Budget cuts forced the hospital to let some of its staff go, and as usual nurses were the first to go. I'd been working at Heartland General since I graduated nursing school and was shocked that I was one of the first to be let go. Especially considering I'd been there longer than half the other nurses. But such is life. As much as it sucked, my only option was to roll up my sleeves and find another job. Only, finding another nursing position was impossible in this small town. I spent weeks looking, and the only place to give me a call back was a small clinic thirty minutes outside of town, and the only thing they could offer me was part-time. And when you have bills to pay and a kid to take care of, part-time isn't going to cut it. I was close to giving up hope when Avery, a good friend and nurse I worked with at Heartland who had also been laid off, called to see if I'd found anything. When I told her I hadn't had any luck, she told me about the hospital she was hired at a couple of weeks ago that was in desperate need of nurses.

The only drawback is this hospital is in New Orleans. Avery is from New Orleans and decided to move back home after the cutbacks. After a second conversation with Avery the next day, she put me in contact with her manager. Moving to New Orleans was looking like my only option. Then, after I sent over my resume and had a video call with Edith, my new supervisor at Hopedale who hired me on the spot, the decision was made. I was moving to New Orleans.

"It's a big change for all of us." Aunt Maggie's face goes soft.

"I know," I whisper and wrap my arm around the woman who is not just my aunt but is more like a mother to me. When I ended up pregnant at eighteen and life decided to shit all over me, Aunt Maggie and her wife June were my saving grace. I would not be where I am today without them. I owe them everything.

Pulling away, Aunt Maggie looks at me then wipes away my tears. "Dry your face, child. There will be no more tears," she orders, her voice stern, but I don't miss the way she's fighting to keep her own emotions in check. "You know what I always say?"

"Everything happens for a reason. Trust in the Lord, and he will send you on the right path." I nod.

"That's right. And I happen to have a good feeling about this new adventure of yours. I can feel it in my bones."

I've always trusted Aunt Maggie's 'feelings.' She has a sense about these things and is never wrong.

"Now." She braces her hands on my shoulders. "Go talk to our girl while June and I finish loading the car."

Nodding, I take a deep breath and then trek down the driveway, around the house, and into the backyard. Aunt Maggie and Aunt June live way out in the country where the closest neighbor is a mile away.

My aunts live simply. Aunt Maggie always said all she needed was the tools God had given her. She and Aunt June grow most of their own food, and they make decent money by selling what they don't need down at the farmer's market, along with their canned preserves. It's not like they live off-grid or anything extreme. They just prefer a quiet life. And though they keep to themselves most of the time, the townspeople like and respect them.

Unfortunately, things were not always like that for my aunts. Aunt Maggie is my father's sister, and my dad, along with my grandfather and grandmother, disapproved of Aunt Maggie and who she chose to love. And when she refused to bend to their ways, she left. She chose Aunt June above all else, and she still says it was the best decision of her life. And though I hardly ever saw Aunt Maggie growing up because my father didn't allow it, she didn't hesitate to take me in when I showed up on her doorstep eighteen and pregnant. That's the kind of people my aunts are. Aunt Maggie is so different from my father. Aunt Maggie is warm and loving. She and Aunt June are not afraid to express their affection toward those they love, either.

Growing up, I experienced the complete opposite. My mother was not hearts and rainbows. She didn't read bedtime stories, take me to the park, or teach me about makeup. And my father was too busy working eighty hours a week. I think he sometimes forgot he had a family. I was also an only child. My mother was an only child, so there were no cousins to play with. I often wondered growing up why my parents even had a kid. But I feel like having shitty parents taught me how not to be when it comes to raising my own child. I spend every day making sure my daughter knows she is wanted and she is loved.

When I round the edge of the house, I make my way toward the treehouse at the edge of the property where it's partially blocked by a large oak tree. I can barely make out the two legs draped over the edge of the treehouse, dangling in the summer breeze, but I can hear the sound of a guitar. Twigs snapping beneath my feet alert my girl to my approach and her head turns in my direction. I take in the sullen look on her face, making my heart ache. Taking my daughter from the only place she's ever lived, and all she knows, was not an easy decision.

Kicking my flip-flops off, I climb up to the treehouse. When I clear the last step, I come face to face with my daughter's cat, Fleetwood. I give him a scratch under his chin before crawling the rest of the way inside the treehouse. "Hey, Ladybug."

"Hey," she whispers back, not looking at me as she strums her guitar.

"What are you doing up here?"

She shrugs. "Just thinking."

"Yeah." I nod, putting my arm around her shoulder and pulling her toward me.

"Do we really have to go?" she asks.

"Hey, look at me." I twist, making my daughter look me in the eyes. "I know right now this seems like the worst thing in the world to you. Leaving Aunt Maggie and Aunt June, leaving school and your friends, leaving this place, but this is something we must do. Change doesn't have to be a bad thing, Ladybug. It can even be exciting if you let it."

"It doesn't feel exciting." Her voice trembles.

"I'm sad too. And I'm going to miss this place as much as you, but I'm not focusing on that. Instead, I'm choosing to focus on the positive."

"What positive, Mom? I don't see anything positive about moving away from our home just so you can start a new job. Maybe if you try looking again for something here."

I shake my head. "We talked about this already. It's been more than two months. There are no nursing jobs here. And I can't expect Aunt Maggie and Aunt June to take care of us forever. You have to understand that."

"I know, mom. I understand. It's just..." She lets her sentence hang.

I pull her into me again. "I know, baby girl. But I can't do this without you."

My daughter looks up at me with sad but understanding eyes and nods.

"What do you say, Ladybug. Are we in this together?"

Finally, Sawyer gives me a small smile. "Yeah. I'm with you, Mom."

"That's my girl." I kiss the top of her head. "Now gather Fleetwood into his carrier so we can say our goodbyes and hit the road."

THIRTY MINUTES AND MANY TEARS LATER, I GIVE MY AUNTS ONE final hug before climbing into my car.

"I packed some cold pop and some fresh banana bread for you

two," Aunt June tells me as she kisses my cheek. "I put it in the cooler on the back seat."

"Thanks, Aunt June." I give her a watery smile.

"Don't forget to check in at every stop," Aunt Maggie reminds me.

"I won't." I stick my arm out the window and wave. Putting the car in gear, I take one last look back at Aunt Maggie, who is standing in the driveway with Aunt June's arm linked with hers as they watch us leave. When I finally tear my eyes away from the people and the places I've called home for the past fifteen years, I look at my daughter, who is sitting in the passenger seat. "You ready?"

Her hazel eyes hold mine for a beat before she answers, "As I'll ever be."

AFTER OUR FIRST THREE HOURS ON THE ROAD, I PULL INTO A REST stop in Mississippi, making sure to park close to the pet walk. "Why don't you take Fleetwood for a walk while I call Aunt Maggie."

"Okay." Sawyer climbs out of the car, opens the passenger door, then pulls the cat from his carrier and latches the leash onto his harness.

Grabbing the phone from my purse, I dial and wait for my aunt to pick it up, all while keeping a close eye on my daughter. I can't help but smirk when she gets a few strange looks from other people as if they've never seen a cat on a leash.

"Hello?" Aunt Maggie answers.

"Hey, it's me."

"Hey. How's the trip going so far? Is the car holding up okay?" she asks.

"We just stopped somewhere in Mississippi. The car is good.

I'm keeping an eye on the gauges." My car is a piece of crap, but by some miracle, the old thing is still getting me from point A to point B. I've had the old Toyota since I finished nursing school. Aunt Maggie and Aunt June got it for me as a graduation present, so though it doesn't look like much, it's never let me down. Aunt June had new tires put on it for me last week and had the oil changed. A few months ago, I was having issues with it running hot, and it took a massive chunk of my savings to get it fixed. The mechanic shop guy warned me the fix was only temporary and that what my car needed was a new engine. But there is no way I can afford something like that, not without cutting into my moving funds. I just hope and pray the old girl doesn't fail me for at least a few more months. I'll be making more money, almost twice as much as at Heartland, so I plan to save enough money for a down payment on something more reliable.

"Good, good," my aunt says.

"Listen, I need to use the bathroom and get back on the road. I want to make it in before dark. If I don't call you at my next stop, I'll call when we get there."

"Okay, Jo. Be careful and tell Ladybug I love her."

"I will. Love you, Aunt Maggie."

"Love you too, sweetheart."

Fifteen minutes later, I pull out of the rest area and back onto the highway. "Hey, Ladybug. Reach into the back and get us a couple of sodas, will ya? Aunt June packed some away in the cooler. I think she said something about banana bread, too."

"Sweet," my daughter chirps.

While the two of us eat some banana bread, I decide to kill the silence by turning the radio on.

"Oh, I love this song." My daughter smiles as Stevie Nicks' soulful voice spills from the speakers. She then closes her eyes and does the thing I love most in this world; she sings along to the lyrics of "If You Ever Did Believe." My daughter's voice is like the sun kissing your face on a chilly Autumn day. It's like catching a glimpse of a rainbow after a summer storm, like swaying on the porch swing while listening to the tree frogs croak at sunset while drinking a cold glass of sweet tea, and like having an angel whisper in your ear that everything is going to be alright.

3

FENDER

The alarm on my phone cuts through the steady humming of the oscillating fan beside the bed. I yawn, prying my heavy eyelids open, and stare up at the ceiling. Reaching over to the bedside table, I swipe the bright screen to silence the alarm. My body protests, feeling the muscles at my side pinch as I sit upright. "Fuck," I hiss, my hand pressing against my ribcage. That bastard last night really got me good. I drag my ass out of bed and into the bathroom, where I flip the overhead light on and peer into the mirror over the bathroom sink. The side of my ribcage is dark shades of red and purple from the impact of the barroom chair. Once Wick returned after he and Everest followed the other MC out of town, he checked me over. No broken ribs, but I'll be bruised and sore as fuck for a few days. I reach into the shower, turning the water on, and let it warm before stepping beneath the spray. The instant the hot water soaks into my skin, my body relaxes. My mind begins racing with a million thoughts, but the most overheard ones have to do with the fight that broke out last night at Twisted Throttle, and with my mom. Wick and Everest watched the bikers exit the interstate, heading southeast toward

Mississippi, and lagged behind, continuing to follow them for several miles before turning around. The whole vibe those fuckers gave off didn't sit right with me, nor the rest of the brothers.

I roll my shoulders as the water pelts at my back. Then there's Mom. My sweet mother is battling breast cancer for the second time in her life, and it's taking a much harder toll on her. The chemo treatment is much more intense than she dealt with previously. I tried convincing her months ago, when she first learned the cancer had returned, to move back to New Orleans with me. Still, she refused, saying she would be happier staying put, and she made it clear when I mentioned making a temporary move back to Tennessee that idea was out of the question as well. To ensure she wasn't alone through any of the processes, she enlisted her best friend Amelia, who never thought twice about moving in with my mom. Her friend lived alone. Amelia's husband of almost thirty years passed away five years ago after losing his battle with pancreatic cancer. Mom was her pillar of strength during a heartbreaking time in life, and now she's there when I'm not to do the same for mom. Those two grew up together. Amelia has been my peace of mind for the past few months. She's at my mom's side when I can't be, which I make damn sure I am every chance I get. Once a week, I make that eight-hour drive to lay eyes on her. Unfortunately, each time, her diagnosis remains the same. The cancer isn't responding as doctors would like.

The first time she battled breast cancer wasn't long after I settled here in New Orleans. The doctors performed a lumpectomy and removed some healthy tissue. The cancer cells were isolated to the tumor and hadn't spread anywhere else. Then Mom endured chemo and a round of targeted radiation, since the cancer was sizable enough to suggest an increased risk of recurrence. In the end, it all resulted in a cancer-free diagnosis.

Her body was put through hell the first time, but she won the battle.

Mom went several years cancer-free before the life-sucker returned. This time, with a vengeance. She found the lump herself, then several more tests determined the cancer cells had spread to other parts of her body and were more aggressive. So, her treatment will be as well. Mom and the doctors are determined to beat the monster once again.

A SHORT TIME LATER, I'M PULLING THROUGH THE CLUBHOUSE GATES. After the shitshow last night, Riggs called church this morning. I notice most brothers are already here, aside from Kiwi, who arrives as I dismount my bike.

"Hey, brother," Kiwi says after cutting his engine.

"You look like shit."

Kiwi runs his fingers through his hair. "Piper rescued a litter of pups off the side of the road a few days ago. Some piece of shit left them in a tattered cardboard box." We head for the front door. Reaching out, I pull it open. "Their eyes don't look to have been open long. With no momma dog to nurse them, she's hand-feeding the poor things. And they let you know at all hours when they're hungry."

I chuckle. "Well, look at it as practice for the future when you and Piper decide to have kids."

"We definitely are in no hurry to become parents," Kiwi states as we walk into church and take our seats at the table where the others are waiting. "At least not until after Piper finishes vet school."

Prez begins. "Now that we're all here, let's get down to business. We need to keep our eyes open for retaliation from these Reaper's Nomads. I made a few calls this morning to some of the MC's we know in the surrounding states. I wanted to see if they've heard of these fuckers and what they know about them." Riggs takes a drink of the coffee sitting in front of him, then sets it back on the table. "Hawk over in Texas reported having a run-in with these assholes two months ago."

"I wager they leave a pile of shit to clean up no matter where they go," Wick grumbles. "Last thing we need is another MC causing trouble and leaving a shit stain on our city."

"Did Hawk give details?" I ask.

Riggs shakes his head. "Just that they dealt with the problem and the fuckers moved on, but he warned that these bastards give zero fucks encroaching on someone else's turf."

"What's the game plan?" Wick asks.

Riggs scrubs his beard. "Pay attention. Talk with our connections throughout the city. Have them keep their eyes and ears open."

My phone rings, interrupting church, and Riggs eyes me. One of the rules at the table. No devices while church is in session, but lately, because of my mom's health, Prez has made an exception. Still, I wait for him to give me the go-ahead before reaching into my pocket. It's Amelia's number instead of Mom's, and my heart drops to the bottom of my stomach. My face must mirror my reaction because after swiping the screen and placing the phone at my ear, I lift my head to find my brothers staring at me, their expressions tight with concern.

"What's wrong?" I ask because she hardly ever calls.

"Everything is fine," she says, and my shoulders lose some of the tension they hold. "Your mom is really exhausted and asked that I call." Her pause is too long, and I know there's more she isn't saying. "Sawyer, if you can, you should make your weekly trip a couple of days early. Your sweet momma needs to see you."

I swallow hard. Amelia's words say so much without revealing much. I'm not like my mom. She's optimistic and refuses to see the darker side of her cancer struggles. Me, on the other hand—

knowing begins settling in my bones. I look at the watch on my wrist. "I'll be there before nightfall."

"Thank you, Sawyer." Amelia sighs. The slight wobble in her voice causes a stir of emotions, and I fight like hell to keep them at bay.

"Can I talk with Mom for a moment?"

"She's asleep, hun. I think it's best we let her rest until you arrive," Amelia says. "I'll make dinner. How does fried chicken, buttermilk biscuits, gravy, mashed potatoes, and turnip greens sound?" I close my eyes at the sound of Amelia struggling to hold back emotion.

"Sounds good. I'll see you soon." I slip my phone away. The room is quiet—almost too quiet for my liking. Everyone is fixated on me, waiting. "I need to head out if I'm going to make it to Tennessee before dark."

"Your mom alright?" Riggs asks.

"She's still with us, brother." I take a deep breath. "Can you spare Everest to help Kiwi over at the tactical store? The delivery truck is due in an hour, and the range is booked solid all day."

"We've got everything covered, brother. You get your ass up there to your mom. Don't keep us in the dark. Let us know what's goin' on, yeah?" Riggs states, and I stand. "We're here if you need us."

I glance around the table. "I'll check in later."

I waste no time, leaving the clubhouse and racing like hell back home. It doesn't take long for me to pack a few things in a duffle bag that I strap onto the back of my bike. Then I'm back on the road, nowhere near mentally prepared to be lost in my head for eight hours.

THE SUN IS JUST STARTING TO SET WHEN I MAKE IT TO MY MOM'S house. I travel down the long dirt road leading to her quiet country home. The small farmhouse isn't much to some, but the single-level, white, 2-bedroom 2-bath home with a wrap-around porch is a mansion to my mom. I bought it for her several years ago. I reflect on my success as the house comes into view and take in the free-range chickens running the yard. I've sold many songs over the years, some of them becoming number one hits for various country artists. My dream of singing the music I write didn't develop the way I imagined it would, but that of millions listening to it is still alive, just being shared by others. To date, my biggest accomplishment is taking care of the one person who has sacrificed everything, raising me on her own. If I'm ever only proud of one thing, it's being able to give all this to my mom.

I roll my bike to a stop and park beneath the massive oak tree in the front yard. The tree branches reach far, shading the front of the home, though its leaves are starting to change from green to the fall colors of orange and red. Walter, Mom's five-year-old red bloodhound, lifts his head and bellows but can't be bothered to move from his sleeping spot on the front porch. His old-man name suits the lazy canine. I grab my bag from the back of the bike and make my way toward the house, where I bend down, rub Walter behind the ears, then step over him, pull the screen door open, and walk inside. The smell of fried goodness causes my stomach to grumble.

"Sawyer, is that you?" I hear my mom call.

"Yeah." I toss my bag on the couch.

"We're in the kitchen, sweetie," she says, and I stroll through the living room. I find Mom sitting at the small kitchen table, with a shawl wrapped around her shoulders and a scarf covering her bald head. Amelia sets a bowl of greens next to a plate piled high with biscuits.

"Sawyer." She opens her arms to give me a hug, and I embrace her. "It's always good to see you."

"How you doin'?" I ask.

"I'm good, baby. Go on and sit down." Amelia ushers me toward the table, where I bend to give my mom a kiss against her temple.

"Hi, Mom." I take a seat beside her. She sighs, knowing I need her to spill what she needs to say. She smiles at me. I take her in for a beat, her eyes a little red and the circles beneath them a bit darker than last week when I saw her.

"I'm stopping treatment."

Her statement is like a punch in the gut. No lead-up. No words to soften the blow. Not that I would expect any less from her. Mom has never been one to beat around the bush about things. She's always to the point, but I still protest. "Maybe there's something else the doctors can try. A clinical trial or something."

Mom shakes her head. "I don't want any of it, sweetheart."

"Mom."

"I want to live what bit of life I have left free of chemo. Free of being sick all day." She takes hold of my hand. "It's okay."

Not one damn thing about this is okay. I don't dare speak my thoughts. I keep them to myself because she doesn't need my negativity. "I know it's hard, but this is the right choice for me, Sawyer."

"I'm moving back," I tell her.

"There's no need for that," Mom says, then Amelia sits at the table and speaks up.

"Genevieve."

"No." Mom shakes her head. "I don't need anyone uprooting their lives for me."

"Woman." Amelia gives my mom a stern look. "You dropped everything for months after my Ray passed away to help me navigate life and learn to live without him. You spoon-fed my ass for two days straight because I was such a basket case after we buried him, then picked me up and gave me the strength I didn't have to get my ass out of bed. You did that for me—without hesitation."

"You're here returning the favor, and I'm grateful, Amelia, but I don't want my son uprooting the life he's built to come home and watch me die."

"It's not like you're dying tomorrow. Besides, that's his choice, Genevieve," Amelia says to mom.

"I'm right here," I speak up, feeling forgotten. "Mom, I can appreciate all the reasons behind what you say, but the fact is, I'm either moving in with you, or you're coming home with me." Having said my piece on the matter, I wait for Mom to respond.

"I want everyone's life to move along as if nothing is wrong. I don't need anyone walking around acting like they're waiting for me to die. Hell, I'm not. I'm living. I'll continue to live until my last breath. You have a life back in New Orleans, Sawyer, and a day-to-day job, along with your club. Being here will take away from all of it, and I don't want that."

"Then you'll move in with me. My house is plenty big enough. You'll have your own room and everything. Either way, I'm taking care of you."

"Genevieve. We've talked about this. You need to be with Sawyer. Besides, a change in scenery will do you good." Amelia smiles.

"Okay—fine. I wouldn't mind watching the sunset over the lake. But I can't leave everything unattended here." Mom finally yields.

"If it's alright with you, I'd like to stay," Amelia says. "I'll look after the chickens and house." Mom begins to cry, which she doesn't often do in front of others. Then she faces me.

"You know I can't leave Walter."

I smile. "Yeah, Ma, I know." I lean and embrace my mom. "I'll take care of you both."

"I'm getting in on this." Amelia sniffles, gets up from her chair, and throws her arms around us. "Damn, you are one stubborn woman." Amelia pulls away and wipes her eyes with the collar of her shirt. "Now then, let's eat."

We spend two hours filling our stomachs with a home-cooked meal and our spirits with conversation about anything but cancer or death.

Mom tires out not long after dinner and goes to bed. Amelia spreads a sheet over the sofa, then lays a pillow and blanket down. "Going home with you is the best thing for her, but I'm going to miss her company every day."

"You're more than welcome at my home anytime," I reassure her and turn the TV on to find a movie to numb my mind. I plop down on the sofa and take off my boots. "She pretty much decided this a long time ago, didn't she? That if all of it didn't work, she wasn't going to fight it anymore?"

"Yeah." Amelia sits in the nearby chair. "She's been talking about it for a while now. Your mom prepared for the worst but hoped for the best, honey. She really did." We sit silently for a beat, then Amelia stands. "I'll let you rest. Goodnight, hun."

"Night." I wait until she walks out of the living room before placing a call to Riggs.

"Hey, brother. How's it goin'?"

"Nothing the doctors are doing is working, and Mom has decided to stop treatment."

"Shit, man. Sorry to hear it. They give her a time frame?"

I rub my eyes. "She didn't say, and I haven't asked yet."

"Anything we can do?"

"No, brother. I'll be here for at least another day or two to settle a few things, then I'll rent a trailer to haul my bike and whatever my mom wants to bring back, because she is coming home with me." I sigh and feel a headache forming at the base of my skull. "There is one thing. I will order some furniture for the extra bedroom downstairs and have it delivered, hopefully before returning. Could you have one of the brothers there at my place tomorrow?"

"You've got it."

"Thanks, brother."

"No thanks needed. We always do for one of our own." Riggs says before ending the call.

———

A COUPLE OF DAYS LATER, I'M SITTING AT THE KITCHEN TABLE WITH Mom and Amelia, eating breakfast before I head into town and rent a trailer large enough to transport my bike and the few things my mom is bringing to New Orleans. "You sure you'll be alright out here all by yourself, Amelia?" Mom asks.

"You stop worrying about me, now. I'll be just fine." Amelia lays her hand on top of my Mom's.

"I just feel so guilty leaving you behind. It's not right. Not after all this time you've taken care of me. Maybe I should stay." Mom sounds torn.

Amelia shakes her head. "Nonsense. You need to be with your family."

"You are my family too." Mom's voice breaks.

"Yes, we are. Genevieve, you're the best friend I've ever had. More than that, even. You are my sister. But your time now is better spent with Sawyer. I'll take care of the house, and those mean-ass chickens." They both laugh, and Amelia adds, "I'll come to see you in a few weeks."

"What would I do without you?" Mom looks at her best friend with watery eyes and a warm smile.

The rumble of motorcycles halts the conversation. "What in the world?" Amelia stands and walks to the window over the kitchen sink, facing the long dirt driveway leading up to the house. "We have company." I push my chair from the table, stride over to the same window, look outside, and see three bikes and a truck coming down the road. I shake my head.

"Who is it?" Mom asks.

"The club." Turning on my heels, I head for the front door and step out onto the porch. Riggs, Wick, and Kiwi pull their bikes up close to the house. Nova parks the truck a few yards away. Riggs dismounts his bike and strolls up onto the porch. "Prez?" I look at him confused and look at the others, then back at him. "What's going on?"

"We're here to help." He spreads his arms. "We're gonna help haul your momma's things back to New Orleans. Nova will drive your bike back home, and you and your momma will travel back in his truck."

'I don't know what to say, brother." I look at every one. "Thank you."

"Riggs." At the sound of my mom's voice, I turn to see her and Amelia standing in the open doorway.

"Mrs. Huntington." Riggs moves toward her. "How ya been, sweetheart?" He hugs my mom.

"I'm hanging in there." She smiles at him. "It's been too long since I saw you."

"Yes, Ma'am, it has," Riggs agrees. Ever since Mom has known Riggs, she's had a sweet spot for him.

Mom pats his cheek. "Still as handsome as ever."

Riggs grins.

"Well, come on in." She looks at the others, asking, "You men hungry?" and she gets a round of *yes ma'am* from them. "Let me feed you then. It's the least I can do."

A few hours later, close to noon, we have the truck loaded with some of Mom's belongings and the dog. My brothers wait on their rides while Mom says her goodbyes to Amelia. "We'll talk every day. And I'll drive down in a week after you've gotten settled." Amelia pulls Mom in for a hug. They both wipe tears from their eyes, and Amelia follows Mom and me to Nova's truck. I open the passenger door and help Mom climb in. Mom and Amelia share a last look before I close the door.

"You have my number if you need anything. Don't hesitate to call." I hug Amelia. "Got it?"

She pats my back. "Take good care of your momma."

"Yes, ma'am."

4

JO

The sun peeking through the crack in the curtains rouses me from sleep, and the scratchiness of the cheap sheets against my legs reminds me of where I am. I was two hours from reaching New Orleans yesterday when my car decided to shit all over my day. I should have known that, when I told Aunt Maggie all was good, I was jinxing myself. Luckily there was a mechanic shop close by, and they were able to come tow my car to their shop. The older gentleman driving the tow truck was also nice enough to give us a ride to his shop. And it just so happened there was a hotel across the street from the shop, as well.

Climbing out of bed, I look back over my shoulder to still see Sawyer snoozing with Fleetwood in a ball at her feet before I head to the bathroom. The hotel has a no-pet policy so we had to sneak him in. On the way to the bathroom, I snag the plastic bag containing the toothbrushes and toothpaste I bought at the corner store last night. Once I've washed my face and brushed my teeth, I stare into the mirror and look at my pale complexion under the fluorescent light. My eyes have dark circles under them, and my hair looks like a rat's nest and is in need of a wash. I decide to forgo the shower, though, since I don't have any clean clothes to put on. And there is no way I can shower then put the same clothes I was wearing the day before back on. I'll just have to bear it. Instead, I decide to tie my hair into a loose braid, letting it hang down my back.

By the time I emerge from the bathroom, Sawyer is awake and sitting up in bed. "Morning, Ladybug."

She mumbles something that resembles a greeting while rubbing her eyes with the backs of her hands.

"You hungry?" I ask. "I figured we could eat at the little diner down the street before going to pick up the car."

"You think the guy can fix it?" she asks with worry in her voice.

I plaster on a fake smile. "I'm sure he can, honey. But let's not worry about that right now. Right now, I'm thinking about some pancakes and bacon." I wink. "Go get ready while I take Fleetwood out to use the bathroom."

"Okay." Sawyer hops out of bed and dashes off to the bathroom. While she's getting ready, I slip Fleetwood's harness and leash on him, grab my phone from the nightstand, and step outside, locking the door behind me. Peering around to make sure management is not around, I slip around the corner of the hotel toward the tree line on the backside of the property for Fleetwood to do his business. While Fleetwood searches for the perfect patch of grass to leave his pee-mail, I place a call to Aunt Maggie.

She picks up on the first ring. "Hey. Did you make it okay? You didn't call."

Pinching the bridge of my nose, I sigh. "I know. I'm sorry, Aunt Maggie. The car broke down and we had to stay in a hotel last night."

"Oh no. Do you need June and me to come get you? Why didn't you call?"

"No, no. Don't do that. I was able to call a tow. And I didn't say anything because I knew you'd worry. The car is at the shop now, and the guy who owns it said I could stop by around ten this morning to see about it. He thinks it's the alternator. If it is, then he'll be able to get us back on the road today."

"Damn. You sure you'll be okay?"

"Yeah. We're about to head out and get some breakfast now, then I'll go see about the car."

"I don't like the idea of you two being stranded. Maybe June and I should come down anyway."

"No, Aunt Maggie. Don't go through the trouble. We'll probably be back on the road before you get even halfway here. And I'm hardly in the middle of nowhere. I mean, I can literally see the mechanic shop from where I'm standing."

"Well, alright. But I want you to call me the minute you're back on the road."

"I will. Love you, Aunt Maggie."

"Love you too."

An hour later, we're walking out of the diner. My daughter is several paces in front of me with her face glued to her phone and not watching where she's going when a group of guys come walking in. "Ladybug, watch out," I warn two seconds too late, because just then my daughter stumbles and bumps into a large man. My eyes get big when I take in his appearance, and I immediately pull my daughter to my side. The man is over six feet five inches tall, has impressively broad shoulders, and a few days' worth of scruff covers his face. I then take in the leather vest he is wearing with the name patch that reads Grizz.

"I'm so sorry about that. Teenagers and their phones." I give an awkward laugh. "They don't pay attention to much else these days."

The huge man lets out a throaty chuckle that somehow puts me at ease, even though his size and appearance are incredibly intimidating.

"No worries, ma'am."

With a jerk of his chin, the man steps around us and heads inside. A moment later, I watch as four other men wearing the same leather vest as the other guy walk into the diner.

"Man, he was huge," Sawyer whispers as she looks back over her shoulder.

I poke her in the side and shush her. "Be good. And try taking your eyes from your phone while you're walking. Deal?"

My daughter at least has the decency to look sheepish. "Sorry, Mom."

When I walk up to the open bay door of the mechanic shop, the man who helped me yesterday steps out while wiping his hand on a grease rag. "Mornin'."

"Good morning." Shielding my eyes from the sun, I peer up at the older gentleman as he approaches. "I'm here about my car. Please tell me you got her running again."

"Well, I got good news, and I got bad news."

I sigh. "What's the good news?"

"Good news is she's runnin' again."

I let out a relieved breath. "Thank goodness." My shoulders lose some of their tension. "So, what's the bad news?"

"Bad news is I don't think she's got much life left in her. To be honest, I'm surprised she's made it this long."

I look over at my car sitting just inside the shop and bite my bottom lip. A new vehicle is not in my budget and won't be for a few more months. Hell, I will barely be able to pay the bill here. That's going to be another chunk of my near nonexistent savings.

"I'll tell ya what, I already put in a new alternator, but if you can leave the car here with me for a few more hours, I can take care of some of the other issues I spotted while under the hood. With any luck, that will buy you some more time."

I shake my head. "That's really kind of you, but I'm sure something like that will cost more than what I can afford."

The old man holds up his grease-stained hand. "Getting you

and your daughter back on the road and safely to your destination is all the payment I need. You can just pay me for the work on the alternator, and we'll be square."

"I can't possibly," I protest.

The man stops me again. "You come back here in about two hours, sweetheart, and I'll have your car ready to go."

BY NIGHTFALL, I'M PULLING INTO THE DRIVEWAY OF THE LITTLE BLUE house that I rented. I found the listing a couple of weeks ago, and though the neighborhood doesn't look like much, the two-bedroom house was within my price range and close to the hospital. And as I climb out of the car, gaining a better look at our new home, I see why the house was so cheap. The roof is missing more than a few shingles, one of the front windows is missing its shutters, the blue paint on the siding is chipping, and the grass looks like it hasn't been cut in months.

"Mom, are you sure this is the place?" Sawyer comes around the hood of the car to stand beside me.

"Yeah, this is it. Come on." I nod toward the front steps while glancing around our surroundings. The street appears quiet, with a single street light illuminating our house and our neighbor's. A couple of houses down, I can make out a lone figure sitting on the porch, and upon closer inspection, it appears to be an elderly man. "The landlord said he left the keys under the mat." And just like I was told, a single silver key lies under the mat at the front door. Inserting the key into the lock, I turn the knob and am immediately assaulted by the smell of stale cigarettes.

"Mom, it stinks here." Sawyer pinches her nose. Luckily, when I flick the light on, the place doesn't look as bad as it smells. The wood floors are a bit scuffed, and the walls look like they could use a coat of paint, but other than that, it's not too bad.

"Looks like we have some cleaning to do." I shut the door

behind us then do a quick walk-through of the rest of the house. The living room and kitchen are open-concept, and there is a short hallway off the living room that leads to the two bedrooms, the bathroom, and a small utility closet. The landlord did mention a washer and dryer hookup in the detached garage, but I'll be lugging our clothes to a laundromat until I can buy a washer and dryer.

Looking over at my daughter, I take in the deflated expression on her face. Like me, she's not digging our new pad. "Hey." I walk over to her and place my arm around her shoulders. "It's not so bad."

She gives me an 'are you kidding' look.

"I'm serious. It will feel like home in no time. We just have to put our mark on it. You'll see." I give her a squeeze. "Come on. You can help me unload my mattress after you bring Fleetwood in. We'll camp out in the living room tonight. Get a good night's rest. Then we'll hit town tomorrow to pick up cleaning supplies and groceries. Yeah?"

Sawyer gives me a small smile and nods.

"That's my girl." I kiss the top of her head.

5

FENDER

"Another day, another dollar made." Kiwi counts the day's earnings. "People are buying up ammo like they're preparing for a zombie apocalypse."

I lean against the counter, staring at the laptop screen, looking over an invoice before clicking Send. "Yeah, and we'll be feelin' the pinch on products for at least a week. Most of the ammo we're out of is on backorder from the suppliers." I close the computer. "Let's lock shit down and get goin'." I walk from behind the counter toward the office located at the back of the building. Kiwi follows.

"How's your mom settling in, mate?" he asks.

"Adjusting—mostly tired. She's doin' a lot of sleeping." After walking into the room, I set the laptop on the desk and Kiwi strolls over to the safe, punching in the code.

Kiwi nods. "Your mom is a courageous woman."

"That she is." A heaviness presses against my chest. I clear my throat. "I'm gonna turn off the lights and make a final walk-through of the shooting range. Mind grabbin' that bundle of broke-down boxes and tossing them in the bin out back?"

"No problem. Why don't we stop by the bar and have a beer?"

"Naw, brother. I need to get back home."

"No worries. I'll meet you around the front in a second." He gives me a look of understanding.

Shutting the office light off, I step out of the room and close the door. On my way through the building, I check the restrooms and vending machine area. After entering the range area, I make a thorough walk-through, picking up crumpled targets lying on the floor and tossing them into a nearby trash can. Before turning off the lights, I stare down the range field and can't help but give pause and think about Track. It's hard to believe so much time has passed since we found him here, dead.

I stride back to the entrance, my heavy boots trudging against the concrete floor, stirring up an echo with every step. I scan the area one final time, then flip the two switches on the wall, and the shooting range goes dark.

Once outside, I stand beside my car, pull my phone out, then shoot a text to Everest, letting him know he'll be relieved soon. Knowing he's watching over my mom while we see how shit plays out with Reaper's Nomads puts my mind at ease. I shove the phone back into my pocket and light a cigarette. I inhale the nicotine, holding it in until I feel the burn, then release my breath as I glance around the parking lot. One of the lights flickers a few times then goes out altogether. I'll have to get someone out here to replace the bulb. "Damn, Kiwi. What the hell is taking so long?" I grumble, then start making my way toward the back end of the building. Halfway there, the hairs on the back of my neck stand on end. Something doesn't feel right as I near the corner, and I reach for the weapon at my side.

"KILL THE MOTHERFUCKER!" I HEAR A MAN SHOUT, FOLLOWED BY A thud.

At the same time, a loud crack that sounds like shattering glass breaks the night's silence, but I don't have time to investigate. A second crash, the same as the first, quickly follows as I take off in a sprint and round the corner with my gun raised, finding Kiwi going toe to toe with two motherfucking Reaper's Nomads. One of them kicks my brother in the nuts, then pulls his weapon and takes aim while Kiwi's doubled over.

I don't hesitate to pull my trigger before he does.

One bullet and the fucker hits the ground.

The other biker tries running, but Kiwi charges, tackling him to the ground, where he proceeds to beat the bastard unconscious.

"You're a dead man." I spin to find myself face-to-face with the barrel end of a gun, held by another Reaper's Nomad. "Remember me motherfucker?" he sneers, and I take a better look at his face.

"You're even uglier than I remember," I smirk, and his eyes flash with rage. Behind the bastard's back, I catch Kiwi getting to his feet, breathing heavily. The asshole is so focused on me he's neglected the fact we aren't the only men here. Stupid bastard. Kiwi quietly lifts a bat from the ground near the dumpster, which I'm assuming is what they clocked him with when the two jumped him.

"I always get my revenge." The guy spits at my face, his spittle spattering across my cheek.

"Nighty night motherfucker." I do nothing but grin. Then Kiwi cracks the bat across the back of the fucker's skull. His body goes rigid, then limp, and he falls sideways, landing hard on the ground.

I nudge the piece of shit with the toe of my boot. "He's out cold." Then I glance over to the one I shot. He's gone. "We're missing one." I jerk my chin and Kiwi shifts his attention to where the shot biker was. We both search, looking for the bastard, but find no signs of him except for the blood on the ground where he fell. "The coward ditched his brothers to save his own ass." Then I ask Kiwi, who walks over to the pile of shit he beat. "What about that one?"

"He's alive." Then, for the hell of it, Kiwi stomps the son of a bitch between his sprawled-out legs. "Kick me in the dick, motherfucker." He stomps on the guy's balls again. "I'll make sure you never fuck again." He repeats the process a couple more times before backing away. Kiwi searches the ground while rubbing the back of his head. "The asshole clocked me good. My gun is around here somewhere." He kneels, finding his weapon lying on the ground near the chain-link fence at the edge of the property line nearby. "The fuckers got a jump on me."

After disarming the two remaining bikers, I pull my phone out and call Riggs. "What's up?"

"We have a situation, Prez. Kiwi and I have two unconscious Reaper's Nomads on our hands."

"Son of a bitch."

"What the fuck?" Kiwi takes in a deep breath. "You smell smoke, mate?"

That is when I remember the sound of shattered glass from moments ago.

"Shit!" I look at Kiwi while the phone is still in my ear. "They move, shoot them." I take off toward the front of the store, where flames are licking out of the storefront window. "Prez, the building is on fire, but the sprinkler system is doing its job." I move to unlock and open the front door.

"I just got notice from the security company. The fire department is already on the way. Do not go inside, and don't touch anything."

"Fuck!" I take a step back as the heat intensifies. "What do you want us to do with the two assholes we have out back?" I ask.

"I'm on my way. Find a way to get them out of there and to the clubhouse before first responders arrive."

"I have my car."

"Good. I'll deal with everything else. Now go," Riggs barks then he ends the call.

I rush to my car, jump in behind the wheel and drive around back. "The fuckin' store is on fire."

"Shit." Kiwi runs his fingers through his hair.

"Yeah. The good thing is the fire system came on and is helping suppress the flames. Bad news, the fire department and police will be swarmin' the place soon." I open the trunk, then grab one of the bikers by the feet. "Come on. Prez says take them to the clubhouse." Kiwi helps lift the biker, and we toss him in the trunk. We do the same with the other guy, but we struggle to get the second piece of shit stuffed into the trunk of my car. I close the lid and lock it. "Let's go." I hop back in the running vehicle and Kiwi jumps into the passenger seat. Riggs and Wick pass us by as we pull away from the tactical store, both giving nods, but neither stops.

Once at the clubhouse, I park, climb out and stride to the back end of the car. Kiwi draws his weapon as I open the trunk. Two sets of eyes stare down the barrel of my brother's gun. "Move." I order them to climb out, and they do as they're told. "Now strip."

"Fuck you." The bearded one spits. My hand shoots out, grabbing a fist full of his hair, then I slam the side of his head against the edge of the open trunk.

"I said, strip."

He grits his teeth, then shrugs his cut off, followed by his boots and the rest of his clothes. His friend reluctantly does the same. "Start walkin'." Kiwi shoves one of them in the direction of the shed. It's dark when we step inside the concrete structure. The musty, damp smell from the mighty Mississippi close by seeps through the cracks between some bricks. I flip the switch on the wall, and the small dim light over my head flickers on, and I can hear the dripping water from the leaky faucet hitting the concrete floor. I walk to the other side of the room and start pulling on a heavy chain, lowering a large hook down from the metal ceiling beams once used to hoist motors out of semi-trucks. Kiwi grabs some rope nearby and tosses it at one of the bikers. "Make yourself useful and tie your friend's wrists and ankles together." The rope lands at the man's feet.

With the guy bound, Kiwi places the hook in position. Reversing the direction, I pull down on the chain again, hoisting the bastard with his bound hands above his head until his feet leave the floor.

"Where do you want this one?" Kiwi asks, his gun trained on the other biker.

I step up to the Reaper's Nomad whose name patch is in my pocket. "String him up with his brother." I smirk.

Wick and Riggs arrive almost two hours later while Kiwi, and I relax outside, smoking. "What's the damage?" I ask, flicking the cigarette to the ground and snubbing it out with the toe of my boot.

Riggs sighs. "Damage was contained to the storefront. Luckily most of the ammunition we carry is located toward the rear wall, and the fire hadn't reached that area. All our clothing merchandise is gone, along with some rifles and display cases. Insurance should cover most of the inventory lost as well as structural damage, since this was arson."

"They determine what started the fire?" Kiwi asks.

"Not yet." Wick shakes his head.

"Where's Nova?" I ask.

"He's with the women at my place until we get done here." Riggs jerks his chin. "Now, what do ya say we get started."

IT'S NEARING MIDNIGHT, AND KIWI LANDS ANOTHER BLOW TO ONE OF the fuckers hanging from the motor hoist. At the same time, I deliver some pain of my own on the other by pulling off another fingernail, leaving him with a matching set of bloodied digits. I toss the needle nose pliers in my hand to the side.

Both men are beaten and bloodied. We've been going back and forth with the two pieces of shit all night, and neither is yet to give up their club's location.

"Prez. Neither is breakin'," Kiwi says lighting a cigarette.

"I say we off both and head home to our women," Wick suggests.

"Which one has the higher rank out of the two?" Riggs strikes a match along the brick wall and lights the cigarette he's holding.

"This one," I grunt, and pull the bastard's patch from my pocket that I took from him the other night. Riggs turns it over in his hands. He flicks ashes onto the floor and eyes the bastard. "Willin' to talk?" Riggs holds the burning end of his cigarette close to the guy's eye. His teeth chatter from the temperature, which is the same as outside, dropping into the low forties.

"Go fuck yourself." He spits blood at Riggs face. Bad move. Riggs snubs the cigarette out using the fucker's eye socket as an ashtray. The pussy roars in pain.

"I think what the Reaper's Nomads need is another lesson in respect." Riggs pulls a bandana from his back pocket and cleans his face. "And you, being their Vice President, get to teach your President this valuable lesson."

The guy laughs manically. "We aren't goin' anywhere. My club will kill you and your men. Then we'll take your city and your women."

Riggs just looks at him, unfazed by his threats. I like that about him. It's what makes him a damn good leader. Riggs is skilled at keeping his cool. "We will never bend to your demands, and I won't deliver any message."

"Oh, you won't need to deliver any message." Riggs looks at me.

I nod, pull my weapon from the holster, and shove the barrel down the bastard's throat. His eyes widen, and he jerks his head from side to side. I grab hold around his neck, and the poor motherfucker stops thrashing then proceeds to piss himself.

I chuckle at his expense and say, "You are the message, motherfucker," and pull the fucking trigger.

I step away from the dead man and holster my weapon. Riggs looks at his watch. "Let's clean this shit up. We'll dump the corpse and his friend outside city limits for their club to find."

One thing you don't do is threaten our women.

6

JO

I woke up at the butt crack of dawn this morning to get an early start on cleaning up the yard before the heat becomes unbearable, but the stupid mower I found in the garage has been giving me fits. "Come on, you stupid son of a bitch." I pull on the starter cord to the lawnmower for the hundredth time, making it sputter to life. "Finally," I mutter. Pushing my weight forward, I trudge along behind the machine as it kicks up grass and flings tiny bits of debris at my legs, reminding me I should have worn pants.

With the last patch of grass cut, I kill the mower and use the back of my hand to wipe the sweat running down my forehead. The New Orleans heat is no different than Tennessee's, though the humidity here is brutal. I'm guessing that has something to do with being so close to the river. And I'm not going to get started on mosquitos or the fact that the temperature can drop to the forties overnight then climb back into the eighties the next day. Leaning forward, I brush the grass off my legs, then a movement out the corner of my eye catches my attention. I watch as the guy who lives next door steps out of his house with a beer in his hand. Jesus, it's not even ten in the morning yet. The creepy dude has been sitting in a chair on his porch watching me since I started cutting the grass. I've been out here for two hours, and this is the third beer I've seen him down. At first, when I saw him, I offered a polite smile, but as the minutes ticked by with him watching me, his presence has done nothing but make me uncomfortable. I mean, the guy is not even subtle about watching me or the way he has constantly been grabbing at his crotch.

I take another glance in his direction, taking in his pudgy tummy and white, sweat-stained t-shirt. This time he catches me looking and gives me a chin lift while lifting his beer to his lips. Deciding this is not a man I want to be friendly with, I ignore him and go about putting the mower away. Not wanting to risk seeing the creep again, I store the lawnmower in the detached garage and then slip back in the house through the back sliding glass door. When I walk inside, I see Sawyer sitting at the table eating a bowl of cereal. "Morning, Ladybug."

"You should have woken me up. I would have helped cut the grass," she says around a bite of food.

Walking over to the sink, I wash my hands. "It wasn't so bad. Besides, you worked hard yesterday helping me clean this place and unload all our stuff."

"Yeah, but you worked just as hard. And we're supposed to be a team." She gets up from the table, walks over to me, and places her empty bowl in the sink. Her words sink in as I look around the kitchen and living room, seeing all we accomplished yesterday. The furniture we have is not much, and it's not brand new, and nothing matches, but it's us. Everything was bought second-hand before we moved except for the old rocking chair that sits in the corner of the living room. The chair belonged to Aunt Maggie and is the same chair I spent hours rocking Sawyer in when she was a baby. When Aunt Maggie was helping me pack, she insisted I take it. Thinking about those memories of holding my baby girl in my arms and the many sleepless nights we shared, or the times she was sick and the only way to soothe her was to spend hours rocking her, starts to bring up other memories. Memories of a time when I thought love was the answer to all my problems. A love I thought was unbreakable. Boy, was I wrong! Love can only be found in fairytales. I learned the cold, hard truth about love the hard way.

Shaking the foggy past from my brain, I dry my hands on a dishtowel and pull my daughter in for a hug. "You're the best, you know that?"

She winds her arms around my waist. "I am pretty awesome, aren't I." She giggles when I tickle her side.

"You're a mess is what you are." I laugh. "What do you say we go into town and treat ourselves to a Mani-Pedi today?" I saw a place when we were out getting groceries yesterday. Visiting the salon is yet another luxury I can't afford, but I'd sacrifice anything to brighten my daughter's day and to see a million more smiles like the one she is giving me now.

"Really!" Sawyer perks up.

I smile. "Really. Then we can go pick out a new outfit for your first day of school."

"Yes." She throws her hands in the air. "I'm going to get dressed."

"Be ready in thirty minutes!" I call out when she dashes down the hall toward her room. "I'm going to jump in the shower really quick."

After my shower, I tie my hair back in a loose braid, then slip on a white, long-sleeve casual dress that sits a couple inches above my knees and pair it with some boots. When I walk into the living room, I find Sawyer seated on the sofa with her face glued to her phone, wearing a dress like mine, only hers is a soft yellow. And it's times like this when I look at my baby and realize she's not a baby anymore. My daughter is so beautiful it literally makes my chest ache, with her long dark hair, hazel eyes, and legs up to her elbows. Closing my eyes, I send a silent prayer up to God that my girl gives me a couple more years before she decides she likes boys. That's not likely to happen, though. My girl is fifteen, so I know my impending doom is lurking just around the corner.

THE BELL ABOVE THE DOOR JINGLES WHEN I WALK INTO THE SALON, and a woman with bright red hair greets us. "Hi. Can I help you?"

"Yes. My daughter and I would like to get our nails done," I tell her with a smile.

"Sure, we can do that." The woman gestures for us to come sit in the two empty chairs next to another lady getting her nails worked on. "You two can come to sit over here. I'm Sadie, by the way. And this is my friend, Promise." Sadie throws her hand in the direction of a beautiful brunette who offers a kind smile.

"It's nice to meet you, Sadie. I'm Josephine, but you can call me Jo, and this is my daughter, Sawyer." My daughter offers a little wave.

"Hey there gorgeous." Sadie looks around me at my daughter. "Sit next to Promise, and I'll get started on you. And Mom, you sit beside her and Zackary will take care of you."

At that moment, a guy wearing a pair of ripped jeans, a tie-dye crop top with matching crocks, and a mop of curly blonde hair comes striding out from the back of the salon. "Did I hear someone say my name?"

"You indeed did," Sadie tells him. "Jo needs her nails done."

Zackary looks from Sadie to me with his hip cocked, then gives me the brightest smile. "Are you Jo?"

"I am." I smile back.

"Fabulous! And who is this gorgeous creature with you?" He points a perfectly manicured finger at Sawyer. My daughter bites her bottom lip and turns shy at Zackary's compliment.

"This is my daughter."

"Hi." Sawyer waves at Zackary.

"Stunning!" Zackary claps his hands. "Sadie, we must switch so I can take care of Little Miss here." Zackary looks at me. "Is that okay, Mom?"

"Of course," I tell him. "You good with that, Ladybug?" I ask my daughter, who only beams and nods at Zackary.

"Perfect. I have just the color. It's called Sunshine Melody. It will match that beautiful dress you're wearing."

My daughter's face turns red and she giggles. "Thank you."

"Just speaking facts, Little Miss."

A few minutes later, Sadie sits down in front of me and begins working on my nails. "So, I've never seen you in here before. Are you visiting or living nearby?"

"We actually just moved here."

"Yeah? Where from? If you don't mind me asking. We're a nosy bunch around here." Sadie winks.

I chuckle. "I don't mind. And to answer your question, we moved here from Tennessee."

"What brought you to New Orleans?" This comes from Sadie's friend, Promise.

"My job. I'm a nurse. The hospital I was working at before had a bunch of layoffs, and, unfortunately, I didn't have any luck finding another job close to where I was living. Then a former coworker who lives here called and told me the hospital she works at was looking for nurses."

Promise nods. "Hopedale is a great hospital. I know a couple of the doctors there. I think you'll like it."

"Oh. Do you work there?" I ask.

She shakes her head. "No. I'm a lawyer. My office is just a few blocks from here. I'll give you my card and if you ever need anything, and not just legal-wise but anything in general, feel free to hit me up."

"Um...since you offered, you wouldn't happen to know a

trustworthy vet around here, would you? My daughter has a cat, and I need to have his ear drop prescription transferred, plus he's due for a checkup."

Promise's eyes light up. "I do. My stepdaughter is a vet. I'll give you her name and the address of her office. She would love to have you all over there."

"Your daughter is a vet?" Sawyer perks up. "That's so cool."

"She sure is," Promise says with pride. "You'll love Piper, and she's great with animals."

"Thanks, Promise. I really appreciate the help."

"No problem," Promise says. "A couple of my other friends usually get together a couple times a month for a girls' night. You should come out with us. We planned on going out next weekend."

"Yes! You should come," Sadie interjects.

"I don't know," I tell them.

"It won't be anything crazy. We'll probably just hang out at Twisted Throttle. It's a bar my brother-in-law owns. The place is pretty laid back, and there's live music a few nights a week."

The idea of going out and making new friends does sound appealing. "I'd have to find a sitter."

"Mom," Sawyer groans. "I'm fifteen. I don't need a babysitter."

"Ladybug. I know you can watch yourself, and normally I would leave you home alone, but we just moved here, and I'm not sure I feel comfortable leaving you home alone just yet."

"That's no problem," Promise jumps in. "I can give you the name and number of the sitter who watches my son. Just in case."

"Are you sure?" I usually wouldn't be quick to make those kinds of plans with someone I just met, but my gut tells me Promise is a good person. Sadie, too.

"Of course. Come on, what do you say? Next Saturday. Girl's night."

I mull over the plans in my head for a minute before answering. "You know what, that sounds like fun."

"You ladies are making me feel very left out over here." Zackary cocks his head to the side while eyeing Sadie and Promise.

"Please. You know damn well you're invited to every girls' night, so don't start," Sadie throws back at him.

Zackary waves the emery board in his hand in the air. "Just checking."

THE FOLLOWING DAY, I ARRIVED AT THE HOSPITAL FOR MY FIRST SHIFT just in time. I've since fallen into my new routine and work environment with ease. My co-workers have all been very friendly and welcoming. I've also seemed to catch the eye of one of our residents, Dr. Ledger. His interest hasn't gone unnoticed by the other nurses, either.

"Be careful of that one." Imani waves her fork in the direction of where Dr. Ledger is sitting with one of his colleagues.

I take a break from picking at my chicken salad and look across the cafeteria. "Oh, trust me." I sigh. "The last thing I'm looking to do is get involved with a co-worker. Especially one that has player written all over him."

Imani smiles, her brow lifted. "Are you speaking from experience?"

"Let's just say I made the mistake of dating someone I worked with before, and when things didn't end well, it made our having to work together awkward."

"Pshh. Been there, done that and got the t-shirt, girl."

I laugh. "Don't tell me it was...."

She cuts me off. "Oh, hell no. I wouldn't go near Dr. Ledger with a ten-foot pole. Don't get me wrong, the man is fine with a capital F, but the man has also worked his way through half the nurses in the hospital. Except for the married ones and the ones over fifty."

Dr. Ledger is indeed a good-looking man. Standing at six feet tall, with blond hair and baby-blue eyes, he has that whole heartbreaker look down pat. He's too clean-cut for me, though. I always did like my men to be a little rougher around the edges. Just thinking about my type causes flashes of my past to come rushing to the forefront of my brain, and a pang of the worst heartache I've ever felt washes over me. Not wanting to wallow in those memories, I shake them away.

"Don't look now, but Dr. Playboy is heading this way," Imani murmurs under her breath.

I don't have time to react before Dr. Ledger is standing at our table. "Ladies."

Imani gives him a polite smile. "Hi, Dr. Ledger. How are you today?"

"Doing well, Imani." He then turns his attention to me. "Josephine, I was wondering if I might have a word with you about the patient we saw this morning, Mrs. Broderick."

I sigh inwardly at his use of my full name, even though I've told him several times to call me Jo. "Oh, uh, sure. Just let me throw this away." I go to clean up what's left of my lunch.

"I got it, Jo. You go on ahead." She gives me a knowing look, and I give her one of my own, a look that says I'll get her back for this.

"So, what did you want to talk about?" I ask Dr. Ledger when we stop in front of the elevator. "Was there a change in Mrs. Broderick's care?"

He gives me a sheepish look. "Actually, no. I didn't need to talk to you about a patient. I just wanted to get you alone for a minute so I could ask you something."

My brow scrunches though I have an inkling of what he's about to ask. "Okay. What did you want to ask?"

"I wanted to see if you'd like to go to dinner with me?"

"Oh. I...I don't know. I mean, I just moved to town, and I'm still trying to get me and my daughter settled."

"Of course. I understand you must be really busy."

"Yeah, I'm pretty busy. You know with the move and work. You know how it is." I toss out an awkward laugh.

Dr. Ledger chuckles, showing off his dimples. "Perhaps I'll see how busy your schedule is in a few days."

Damn, this guy doesn't give up. "Sure."

Luckily, his pager goes off, saving me from this conversation. Dr. Ledger looks down at his pager then back to me. "Well, duty calls. I'll see you back in the ER."

"Okay," I say, then watch as he turns and walks off in the opposite direction before disappearing into the stairwell.

7

FENDER

There's been nothing from the Reaper's Nomads MC since we sent one dead and another severely beaten member of their club back to their President a couple of days ago. If war is what they're after, war is what they will get. New Orleans is our city. The Reaper's Nomads are sorely mistaken if they think trying to burn down Kings Tactical after taking Kiwi and me by surprise would make us tuck tail and run.

I shrug a leather jacket over my cut to keep the chill from slicing through me on the ride into town. It's early October here in the south, which means cool mornings and hot afternoons. Not hearing my mom stir all morning, I head downstairs and stop by her bedroom before heading out for the day. I rap my knuckles against the door.

"Come in."

I find her sitting in the recliner beside the bed, with her favorite quilt made by her mother draped across her lap and Walter stretched across the floor at her feet. My chest aches at how frail and thin she's gotten over the past few months. My mom has always been a petite woman, but she's skin and bones now. Not that it takes away from her beauty. Seeing her this way is a slap in the face reminder that cancer is eating her alive. That final round of chemo robbed her body of just about everything she had left to give, though her spirits would never lead you to think so. After all she has been through, my mom is one of the most positive and grateful humans I know. "I'm heading out." I cross the room, brightly lit by the morning sun. Her eyes remain closed, and her body is still. "Mom?"

"Shh." She tilts her chin, seeking the warmth of the sun on her face, and the golden glow it gives her pale skin makes her appear less sickly. "Do you hear that?" I smile, knowing what she'll say next, and come to stand beside her chair, placing my hand on her shoulder. "The angels are singing." She raises her hand, puts it on top of mine, and takes a deep breath. "I'm so grateful to feel and see another sunrise."

I lean down and kiss the top of her head. "Me too." I look out the window at the lake behind my house. "Everest and Payton should be here any minute. Have Payton make you some breakfast."

"I can manage my own cooking, sweetheart. I have enough people waiting on me hand and foot. I need to do things for myself, as long as I'm able. I need to feel normal and less like a person on their deathbed." She lifts the blanket from her lap and, with care, folds it, stands, then lays it over the chair arm.

"Mom."

"Don't mom me, Sawyer. If I'm gonna die, then I'm damn sure doing it on my terms. That means no lying in bed or sitting on my butt all day. If I have breath in my body, I'm living." The mere thought of her dying twists my stomach into knots. "Stop it." My mom's stern yet soft voice scolds me. Raising her hand, she presses her palm against my cheek, her skin cold against my warm skin.

"Stop thinking about the future and focus on today." Her smile calms my thoughts for now.

"Promise you'll rest when needed. Don't overdo it. Payton and Everest are staying all day."

"I promise." Mom stands, wraps herself in a robe, then exits the bedroom. I follow close behind her into the kitchen, where she gathers her herbal mixture and fixes herself a warm cup of tea.

The doorbell chimes, and a moment later Everest and Payton stroll into the kitchen. "Hey, Fender," Payton says.

"Mornin'."

She sets her bag and a sack full of groceries on the kitchen island. "How are you feeling, Mrs. Huntington?"

"Please call me Genevieve. Mrs. Huntington makes me feel so old."

Payton laughs. "You got it. So, you up for baking cookies and binge-watching Outlander on Netflix?"

Mom turns with a mug in her hand. "You had me at Outlander. That Jamie Frasier is delicious."

"And that's my cue to leave." I grab my keys off the counter beside the double doors leading out to the backyard deck. "I'll see you tonight, Mom." I stop beside Everest, who appears a bit irritated. "What has your feathers ruffled?"

He sighs. "Nothin'."

"Oh, he had a run-in with London this morning at the grocery store," Payton is all too eager to supply and Everest grumbles under his breath.

I slap Everest on the shoulder. "Can't help you with that problem, brother. You need me, call."

"Will do." Everest nods.

Once outside, I walk across the yard to a large metal building that houses my vehicles. I roll up the bay door. Inside sit two custom bikes and my 1971 Dodge Super Bee. She was the first car I purchased when I sold my first song. I run my hand over the deep purple finish and think about my journey to get where I am today.

Every plan I had for the future became nothing more than shadows, lost amid uncertainty.

I walk away from the car, then to my bike, and swing my leg over the seat. Things with Jo fucked with my head for a long time. So much of my life and what I wanted to do with it had her in it. It took me a while to unravel her from who I was before pulling my shit back together again. That didn't happen until I settled in New Orleans. Bourbon Street, in many ways, was like going home and playing music on the strip, trying to make something of my music playing for the people in the bars on music row. Crescent City is much rougher around the edges, but its people fed life back into my soul and reignited the flame inside, reminding me I am somebody.

I started saving money and renting a small studio space from time to time for recording tracks. It wasn't anything fancy, just me and my guitar, but I took a chance on myself and began sending in song demos to big and small record labels.

While playing gigs, I put myself out there, letting the world of music know where the fuck I am. That's also around the same time I fell into spending more time with Riggs and the club. Pursuing music never wavered, but I noticed my perspective on life starting to shift, and I wanted the club life as much as I did my music. I just had to figure out how to do both.

I'd been prospecting for Kings for months when I was approached by a record label who wanted to buy the rights for two of the songs I sent in. At first, I was butt-hurt because they only wanted the songs I sang and not me singing them. I'd written those lyrics, and it never occurred to me to want anyone else to sing them. Not until I heard the artist herself sing them for me. It was like she took the heart and soul right out of me and used my emotions but her voice to belt the words. It was then I realized she'd been through some shit herself, and that those songs were just as much made for her as they were for me. The price tag the record label was sticking on the songs was nothing to be passive about. I gave it a bit more consideration before realizing I shouldn't let my ego pass up a great opportunity.

Either way, my music would be on the radio. That was the birth of my musical success. I've sold and written several more songs for various established and upcoming artists since. Even had the chance to play on stage with one a few years ago. My success has made not only my life financially comfortable, but my mom's as well.

I shove my memories aside, start my bike, roll out of the garage, and head for town.

A short time later, I'm pulling into a small mom-and-pop gas station located on a barren stretch of country road between my house and the city. A sweet old couple owns the place, but it's the elderly man who runs things. While filling up, I notice a Harley parked at the rear of the building near the public restroom. I place the gas pump nozzle back on where it belongs and decide to investigate. I keep my attention on the other bike as I walk toward the building. Pulling the entrance door open, I step inside.

Immediately, something doesn't feel right. I scan the inside of the small store, not spotting anyone, including the old man, Mr. Broussard. Pulling my weapon, I begin slowly walking around. When I look back behind the counter where the register is I notice the cash drawer open and empty. *Shit*. I keep moving toward the back of the store. I stop at the door with a small office sign on the front, reach out, turn the knob, and enter the darkroom. Keeping my gun aimed in front of me, I palm the wall feeling for a light switch, then flip it up. "Jesus." The first thing I see is the old man, on the floor, unmoving with blood-matted hair. I rush to his side and check for a pulse. He moans when I touch him. "I got ya, old man."

He cracks his eyes open, flinching when I take a quick look at his head to see where the blood is coming from. "Fender?"

"Yeah. What happened?" I help him into a sitting position.

"Robbed." Mr. Broussard lifts his hand, pointing to the corner of the room where a small safe is open. "He took what I had in the register then demanded I show him the safe. He cracked my head a good one before I could get my gun."

"You have a cut on your head, and I wouldn't rule out a concussion. You need to get to the hospital." I notice the landline phone sitting on the small desk in the room and grab it. "Here. Call the cops. The fucker is still here, out in the shitter. Don't leave this room," I say. Under normal circumstances, I wouldn't call the cops, but Mr. Broussard needs medical attention, and his safety and well-being are more important than me having to deal with the law.

The old man looks up at me after I stand. "Don't get yourself killed."

"Don't worry about me. Now stay put." I cautiously walk back out of the room and close the door behind me. The store is still empty as I make my way to the entrance and step outside again.

The bathroom door swings open, and out stumbles a woman. She falls to the pavement, and the contents of her small handbag scatter across the ground. Then, a man strolls out of the same restroom, his pants undone. He reaches down, plucking a twenty-dollar bill from the woman's belongings. That's when I notice the cut the fucker is sporting: Reaper's Nomads. "Thanks for the refund, you fucking cunt." He laughs cruelly.

"You can't just leave me here. I have no ride!" the woman screeches.

"Not my problem, bitch," he spits. The asshole turns his head in my direction. "What are you lookin' at, motherfucker?" He moves toward me.

I aim my gun at him. "A dead man." His steps are slow and a

smirk appears on his ugly face. "You're one of them Kings bastards." He rubs his hands together.

"That's right motherfucker." I look past him at the half-dressed woman.

"I swear I didn't know he would rob the place and hurt the old guy inside," she cries.

"Get the fuck out of here," I tell her, and she runs back into the bathroom, slamming the door shut. I approach the piece of shit who is glaring at me. "You're not too bright, are you? You Reaper's Nomads are like roaches." The stupid fucker makes a move, and I fire, striking him in the shoulder, but he keeps moving and takes a swing at me. I dodge his fist and land a blow of my own with a left hook to his side. He counters with another wild fist but misses again, stumbling. "Who the fuck taught your sorry ass to fight?" I retake my aim. The asshole rushes me like he's a linebacker and I'm the quarterback, throwing his shoulder and weight into my gut, knocking me off my feet. My weapon is knocked from my hand as I land hard on the pavement. The back of my head strikes the ground hard. The blow momentarily stuns me. "I'm gonna kill you," the guy growls as he straddles me. My eyes focus on him in time to see the blade being pulled from his cut. I roll to the left, trying to avoid the knife, but a hot searing pain radiates across the side of my ribs. The fucker cut me. He slashes at me again, but this time, I'm able to grab his forearm. A struggle ensues. "You kill one of us; we kill one of you!" he grunts, trying hard to gain the upper hand.

Tires screeching pull his attention away enough for me to gain more control of the situation. With a downward motion, I force his hand down, sending the blade into his thigh. The entire blade shaft buries into his flesh, and the son of a bitch growls again. "You son of a bitch!" I swing, my fist connecting with his chin, and his head snaps back. The big fucker rolls off me, and I'm able to get from beneath him. The pain in my side is hard to ignore as I get to my knees. The biker produces a handgun and takes aim at me.

Pop.

A single shot is fired, and the asshole goes down. Looking behind myself, I find Catcher with my gun in his hand. He walks over and helps me to my feet, then hands my weapon over. "You're bleeding." I glance down, and the whole side of my shirt is soaked. I pull apart the slashed cotton, exposing my side to get a better look. The fucker got me good. "Needs stitches," Catcher's deep voice mumbles.

We both look down at the Reaper's Nomad, dead with a bullet between the eyes. "Nice shot," I say, but Catcher says nothing. I face him and clasp his shoulder. "Thanks, brother. I owe you." I glance at my bike, still parked at the gas pump.

"I'll load it on the trailer." Catcher points to his old Chevy, and the flatbed trailer hitched to the back of it. While he loads the Harley and straps it down, I remove my cut and pull the torn shirt from my body. I shrug my cut back on and use my already bloodied shirt to press against the wound at my side. "Listen, I need to check on the old man inside." I hiss at the pain as I apply pressure.

"Get in." Catcher points to his old Chevy. "I'll check on the old man."

I nod. "He's supposed to call the cops. Tell him there's a woman barricaded in the restroom." I grit my teeth, hoisting myself into the passenger seat of his ride. Catcher jogs inside, and it's only a beat before he returns. Without saying anything, he climbs behind the wheel.

"The old man said cops are on the way." He starts the truck. "What about the dead guy?" he asks as he pulls away from the gas station.

"We'll worry about that later."

I've bled through the shirt by the time Catcher reaches the

hospital. He pulls his truck to a jerking stop outside the emergency room doors, causing my body to lurch forward. "Fuck!" I clench my teeth at the searing pain ripping at my side. Reaching across myself, I push open the truck's door and climb out. "Thanks, brother. I got it from here." Then I close the door and walk through the automatic doors as they slide open, where I'm met by a security guard. He eyes me for a beat, his lip curling as he takes in my appearance.

"You gonna be a problem?" the guard asks smugly.

Is this asshole for real? Fuckin' rent a cop. "I've had a shit day. Now is not the time, and I'm not the person to fuck with." The guard squares his shoulders, and just as he's about to open his mouth, I hear a familiar voice.

"Go walk the floors, Hamas," Harold Gloster says. The young guard glares my way before stepping back and walking off. "Sorry about that. Damn newbies always flexing their egos." Gloster's old but lively eyes set on my face, then he notices the blood-soaked shirt I have pressed at my side. "Shit, Fender. It's been a minute since I've seen you here. Go get yourself looked after."

Gloster is a good guy. He's been working security here for a long damn time and is good friends with Abe, Riggs and Nova's granddad.

I move toward the check-in window. "The others should be here any minute."

"They look like you?" Gloster asks.

I chuckle. "No, man. Let my brothers know I'm here."

"You got it." Gloster's voice fades off at the end as he walks outside.

Luckily, I don't have to wait. A nurse walks through the doors leading to the back of the emergency room, her head down, staring at a chart. "Mr. Huntington." The sound of her voice sends a chill up my spine. The moment she lifts her head, it feels like someone sucker punches my gut, knocking all the breath from my lungs. The nurse's lips part, and her eyes widen with surprise. After all this time, she still looks the same—still as breathtakingly beautiful as the last moment I laid eyes on her.

"Sawyer?" My eyes close when she speaks my name. Instantly, flashbacks of that night race through my head. The memories and images so vivid my thoughts transport me back in time. Back to when I thought I had life all figured out. When I was in love. Then the exact moment my heart was ripped from my chest—torn out with her bare hands. All the feelings resurface. Anger, hurt, betrayal, and distrust take root and begin simmering. I open my eyes, letting the emotions glaze over my heart, freezing it solid.

"Josephine." I use her full name, knowing she despises it. The hurt in her eyes is instant, but I tell myself it isn't an ounce of what she made me feel. Jo schools herself and straightens her back.

"Follow me, and we'll get you fixed up." Without saying another word, I fall in behind her. My eyes travel over her body. She's much curvier than she once was, hips a bit wider, breasts larger... I pry my eyes off her shapely ass and remind myself who I'm looking at. "Have a seat on the bed, please." I slide onto the paper-covered exam table. Jo covers her hands with surgical gloves. "I'll need you to remove the vest." The professionalism of her tone sounds forced and her hands shake. "What happened, Mr. Huntington?" Her fingertips touch mine as she lifts the shirt and my hand from the wound. She lets out a soft gasp. "Sawyer." My name slips past her lips again, and I hate to admit I like hearing it.

I swallow hard, trying to focus on a spot of peeled paint on the wall. "Knife." My answer is short.

"A fight?" Jo inquires while assessing the gash. I don't respond, but she never misses a beat. Jo gathers supplies needed to wash and disinfect the area. "You'll need stitches. When was the last time you had a tetanus shot?" She doesn't look up from her task, and I keep my eyes focused forward.

"It's been a while." I keep my tone even.

Jo packs the wound to keep the bleeding to a minimum. "I'll be right back with the shot and the doctor will look you over." Jo discards her gloves, cleans her hands, then leaves the room like her ass is on fire.

Only then does it feel like I can breathe again. What the hell is Jo doing in New Orleans? A knock on the door interrupts my train of thought and a tall, fuck-boy doctor waltzes in. "Mr. Huntington, I'm Dr. Ledger. I heard you had a run-in with a knife." He sits the chart in his hand on the counter, takes a seat on a stool then glides close to me. Jo hands him a pair of gloves, and he smiles at her. My stomach clenches and a fire spreads across my skin. I don't like the way the doctor is eyeing Jo like a piece of candy. I grind my teeth so hard my jaw begins aching. "Thanks, Jo," he smiles.

"It's Josephine." I correct him, my tone hard. The doctor looks at me then at Jo. "Oh, do you two know each other?" he asks, friendly enough with no ill intent, but I don't give two shits at the moment.

"Not anymore," I say at the same time Jo says, "Yes."

The doctor is smart enough to leave well enough alone and moves on. He starts his examination. "It's a clean-cut, Mr. Huntington. It should heal nicely, with minimal scarring." Jo brings the equipment he needs. "What do you say we get you stitched up and on your way?"

I say nothing while he works. I also do my best to avoid looking at Jo. Seeing her after all these years brings more pain than the knife wound. I chance a brief glance in her direction and find Jo's eye's fixated on me. A rush of memories hit me like a ton of bricks, and from the look on her face, she's reliving a few things herself. I tear my eyes away when I begin to feel too much.

"Alright, Mr. Huntington. You're all done. From a few other scars, I see you should know the drill. Keep it clean and covered for a few days. Take over-the-counter pain medication when needed." He removes his gloves then cleans his hands. "Any questions?"

"No." My tone is filled with hate for a man I don't know.

The doctor looks at Jo. He smiles, and I want to punch his face. "He's good to go." Then turns and faces me before walking out of the room. "You take care, Mr. Huntington."

Once he's gone, Jo looks at me. "Sawyer."

"We done here?" I stand, shrugging my cut over my shoulders.

Jo frowns. "I, um, just need to get your paperwork and aftercare instructions."

I brush past her. "Keep it," I sneer, and walk out.

I run into my brothers outside the hospital, gathered in the parking lot by Catcher's truck. "Catcher filled us in on what went down," Riggs says and looks me over. "You alright?"

"Yeah. Just some stitches."

"Church." Riggs orders, then he looks at Catcher. "I'd like you to join us."

Catcher nods then looks at me. "I'll take you and unload your bike at the clubhouse."

A short time later, we arrive at the clubhouse and file into church, leaving Catcher to sit out in the common room with a cold beer. "So, we have another dead Reaper's Nomad to deal with. These fuckers are working my last nerve," Riggs says, irritated.

"What do we do, should the law come askin' questions?" Kiwi asks.

"I've already talked to Mr. Broussard. He has no security cameras, so no evidence you were ever there, and he doesn't plan on mentioning the fact."

Wick looks across the table at me. "Was there only one?"

"Yeah. Him and a woman."

Kiwi leans his forearms on the table. "Did she see you?" he asks me.

"Yeah." I then look at Riggs. "She ran back into the bathroom before the fight began and didn't see anything, but she saw my face."

"Mr. Broussard made mention he was informed of a woman holed up in the restroom, but the cops found no woman on the scene. So, she had to have disappeared before they arrived."

"Was she wearing a property cut?" Nova asks.

"No." I grimace at the pain when moving in my seat. "I don't believe she is associated with the corpse or his club in any way."

Riggs rubs his beard. "We'll make another run before nightfall and see if we spot one of these bastards on our turf."

"Catcher killed that son of a bitch. If it weren't for him, I might not be sitting here now," I say.

"I want to address that." Riggs leans back in his seat and crosses his arms. "Catcher has been hanging around for a few months now. I'd like to offer him a shot prospectin' for the club." Riggs looks around the table. "Vote."

Wick nods. "Approve."

Nova taps the table. "Approve."

Kiwi nods. "Hell yeah, I approve."

Everest folds his arms. "Approve."

I'm the last vote, and my brothers look in my direction. "Approve."

"Alright," Riggs stands and walks to the other side of the room, opening a door. Reaching into the closet, he digs around until he finds what he's looking for. A prospect cut. "Bring him in." Closest to the door, Kiwi stands and pokes his head out, calling for Catcher, who strolls in a few seconds later. "I'm going to get straight to it." Riggs lays the cut with the Kings logo on the back and Prospect along the bottom. "You've expressed interest in the club for a few months now. After what you did today for our brother, we'd like you to prospect." Catcher looks down at the cut then around the room. He's a hard man to read. "Prospecting isn't easy. You'll have to pay your dues and earn the patch. Are you willin' to put in the time and, if need be, bleed for the club?" Riggs waits for a response.

Catcher holds out his hand. "I am."

"Alright, men. Let's hit the street looking for any signs of these fuckers. Afterward, we regroup at Twisted Throttle." Riggs shakes his hand then hands the cut to Catcher. "Suit up."

8

JO

Standing in the shower, letting the hot water wash over me, I can't stop my brain from replaying yesterday's events. I didn't get a lick of sleep last night. Every time I closed my eyes, visions of him kept plaguing me. Sawyer is here. He lives in New Orleans. And is apparently part of some motorcycle club. I'd always wondered what he was doing with his life. I try not to think about it too much because it's a life we were supposed to live together. I keep thinking this is all a dream, that I will wake up and discover what happened yesterday was nothing more than a nightmare. No such luck, though. Because fate has once again decided to shit all over me. Knowing I don't have much time before my daughter wakes up, I bury the hurt that is currently wracking my heart and finish getting ready for my day. Above all else, I can't let my daughter know about the turmoil threatening to wreak havoc on our lives.

"Morning, Ladybug." I turn away from the stove when Sawyer walks into the kitchen.

"Morning, mom." She steps up beside me and kisses my cheek.

"Do you want some eggs this morning? I made plenty."

"Yeah. Eggs sound good. I'll make the toast," she chirps.

"You're in a good mood," I note.

After I got home from work, Sawyer went on and on about the new friends she had made and how she liked all her teachers. I was relieved. I'd spent the whole day yesterday on pins and needles, wondering how she would cope with going to a new school in the middle of the second semester. It's not always easy being the new kid. But the second I stepped through the door after work, she was on me. We spent the evening pigging out on pizza and telling each other about our days.

"Maddy asked me if I want to go with her to the movies and then to the mall on Saturday. She said her mom can take us." Sawyer turns away from the toaster and looks at me with pleading eyes. "I told her I had to ask you first. So, can I please go?"

"I guess it's alright. I want to meet her mom first, and you have to promise to check in."

"Yes!" Sawyer throws herself at me. "Thank you."

I go about scooping some eggs out onto two plates then carry them over to the table. And since Sawyer is busy texting her friend my answer about Saturday, I bump her out of the way with my hip and finish buttering the toast. "Come on and eat before it gets cold, Ladybug."

"Okay."

We sit down at the table when Sawyer pipes up again. "Are you cool with Maddy having a sleepover after the movie? Her mom said it was okay, and she said they would come a few minutes early so you can meet."

I nod. "I think that will be okay."

"Cool." She goes back to texting.

"Thirty more seconds and I want the phone put away." I eye my daughter from across the table. She knows how I feel about cell phones while eating.

"Yes, ma'am." Sawyer gives me a sheepish look then puts her phone down. I agreed a year ago to let her have a phone, but the rules are no phone during meals, and I take it every night before bed.

Twenty minutes later, we're heading out the door. "Did you put your homework in your bookbag?"

"Oh, right." Sawyer jogs down the hall to her room and comes out a second later with her math folder.

"Come on before we're both late." I shuffle out the door, locking it behind me.

On the way to the car, Sawyer leans into my side. "That dude is creepy."

I peer over my shoulder toward the neighbor's house. The man who watched me cut the grass the other day is once again sitting on his porch, a beer in hand and eyes on us.

"He is. Just ignore him." The guy hasn't bothered us since we moved in, but that doesn't mean I'm not going to be cautious. This reminds me that I need to stop by the hardware store for extra locks for the doors and windows. I can't be too careful. My daughter is not home by herself much, but she is home alone for a couple of hours every day after school. She also carries pepper spray, and I keep a taser in the nightstand drawer beside my bed. I have never been one to be comfortable with guns. Aunt June taught me how to use one when I was younger. She was adamant I know how to handle them since she and Aunt Maggie are gun owners and keep them in the house, but beyond that, I don't fool with them.

Climbing into the car, I take a deep breath and pray it starts. When leaving work yesterday, the old girl wanted to act up but came through and got me home. Placing the key into the ignition, I turn. The car sputters for a beat, but thankfully, she turns over. "Thank you," I exhale.

The traffic in New Orleans is not what I am used to, but I managed to arrive at work fifteen minutes early after dropping Sawyer off at school, so I decide to sit in my car and enjoy what's left of my coffee before heading in. It's then my phone chimes with an incoming text.

Promise: Hey. It's Promise. How are you?

With a smile on my face, I reply.

Me: Hi. I'm good. What's up?

Promise: Girl's night has been moved to this Saturday at seven o'clock. Are you down?

Dang. This Saturday is the girls' sleepover. And I won't disappoint my girl by asking her to cancel just so I can go out. But my daughter is always asking for more responsibility. She's always complaining that I don't trust her and treat her like a baby. I saw the truth of it on her face the other day at the salon when Promise offered me her sitter's number. It's not like I'd be staying out late. Lord knows I could use some adult interaction and a couple of hours to decompress from everything that's been going on. I shoot Maddy's mom a quick text with my mind made up, since Sawyer gave me her number before leaving the house. I introduce myself and ask if she'd be okay with the girls being unsupervised for a couple of hours Saturday night and assure her that I would be home no later than nine o'clock. She responds almost immediately, saying that Maddy babysits all the time, and she's totally fine with the girls being home alone for a little while. Two hours tops. With those plans settled, I text Promise back.

Me: Seven is good. I can meet you there.

Promise: Perfect! I'll send you the address to Twisted Throttle.

Me: Great! I'll see you Saturday.

Shoving the phone in my purse, I down what's left of my coffee and mentally prepare myself for the day. Nothing in this world could have ever prepared me for the shock I got yesterday when I walked into that exam room to find the man I once loved more than anything sitting there. And absolutely nothing could have prepared me for the look of hate I saw shining in those beautiful hazel eyes. Once the look of shock was wiped from his face, it was replaced with pure disdain. It was a damn miracle I held myself together long enough to assist Dr. Ledger in stitching Sawyer up. It didn't help that he looked just as handsome as I remember. Sawyer has always been tall, standing at over six feet tall. The most significant difference now is the beard. Oh, God, why did he have to look so good? And I thought he'd have stayed around to find out the answers to the many questions we both obviously wanted to ask, but Sawyer didn't waste any time before putting as much distance between us as he could.

"Stop it, Jo," I chastise myself. "Fuck him." I shake my head. He's the one who walked away without an explanation. If anyone should be mad, it's me. Sawyer Huntington can go to hell.

"Jo! Thank god you're here!" Imani shouts over a flurry of activity the moment I round the corner to the emergency room. "We have a gunshot wound two minutes out."

Diving into action, I toss my purse on top of the desk at the nurses' station and follow Imani to the ambulance bay, where I can hear the sirens in the distance.

Dr. Ledger steps up beside me, offering a curt nod. Gone is the cocky, easy-going guy and in his place is the man I have come to learn, despite his playboy reputation, is a fantastic doctor.

It's been so long since I've gone out with friends that I don't have crap to wear. My wardrobe consists of scrubs, jeans, shorts, t-shirts, and the occasional dress, but not anything that would make me feel sexy. Not that I'm trying to impress anyone. For once, though, it would be nice to feel like a woman and not an overworked mom.

Peering down at my watch, I note the time and curse. "Shit." I

Fender

dig through my closet until I spot a pair of high-waisted, black leather shorts sitting on the top shelf. I bought them two years ago on a whim. I didn't intend to wear them, but for some reason they called to me. Not to mention they make my butt look great. Reaching up, I pull them down and rip the price tag still attached off. Suddenly an idea pops into my head, and I walk over to the dresser, open the top drawer and sift through an assortment of bras until I find what I am looking for. A spaghetti strap, black, lace bodysuit. I dress quickly and pair the outfit with a gold belt and some black and gold, strappy, three-inch heels. After I'm dressed, I run across the hallway to the bathroom, pull my hair up into a high ponytail, put on a little bit of mascara, and top off with some blush and red lipstick. Once I've finished getting ready, I appraise myself in the mirror. "Not bad, Jo," I say to myself.

Looking at the time again, I jump into action. Jogging back into my bedroom, I swipe my small handbag off the bed and hurry out to the living room where Sawyer and her friend watch TV and eat ice cream.

"Wow, Mom. You look hot." Sawyer looks at me with wide eyes.

"Yeah, Miss Gates. Those shorts are killer," Maddy adds.

"Thanks, guys." I grin at the girls.

I grab my keys from the kitchen table. "Remember what I said."

"I know, Mom." Sawyer rolls her eyes. "Lock up behind you, don't answer the door for anyone, check in every thirty minutes, call nine-one-one in an emergency, have a party."

"All right, smartass." I ruffle her hair.

"Seriously, Mom. We'll be fine. Go, have fun for once."

I kiss my daughter's cheek. "You know I love you, kid."

"Love you too."

"I'll be home by nine," I say over my shoulder as I walk out the door.

"Bye, Mother."

I laugh when Sawyer gives me an exasperated glare.

Ten minutes later, I'm pulling into a parking lot across the street from Twisted Throttle. With the directions Promise gave me, the place was easy to find. Climbing out of my car, I take in my surroundings before making the trek across the lot. When I make it to the sidewalk, I note how busy the street is and how many people are coming and going from the bar, and I can hear the soft sound of country music playing as I walk across the street. I smile when I spot Promise standing at the corner waiting for me.

"Hey, you made it," she says and surprises me when she pulls me in for a hug. "You look fantastic, by the way."

I step back. "Thank you."

Promise then introduces me to her friends. First, she gestures to a stunning woman with long, sleek, black hair and eyes the color of gold. "Jo, this is my best friend, London." Next, she introduces me to a woman with wild, curly blond hair and eyes the color of the sea. "And my friend Ruby, and of course you know Sadie."

"Hi." I wave. "It's nice to meet you all."

"You too, Jo. And I love those shorts. You have great legs," London compliments.

"Oh, uh, thank you." I stumble over my words because I'm one of those people who acts all weird when I'm being paid a compliment.

We run into a group of men walking out of the bar, and I see how packed the place is. I turn to Promise. "This place is pretty busy. You sure we'll be able to get a table?"

London waves her hand in the air. "Promise's man works here. We always have a table."

"Oh, wow. That's cool," I say.

"Yeah. Cain's brother owns the place, and he tends the bar a few nights a week." I follow Promise further inside, where she leads the group to a table in the back marked *Reserved*. "This is us."

As we take a seat at the table, a tall, bearded, devastatingly handsome man saunters over, grips the back of Promises' neck, pulls it back, and kisses the hell out of it. The kiss seems almost too intimate for the public and it damn near makes me blush.

"Honey, I'd like you to meet my new friend, Jo. Jo, this is Cain."

Cain reaches his arm out across the table. "Pleasure, darlin'."

We shake hands. "Nice to meet you, Cain."

The handsome man then turns his attention to the other women. "Ladies, the usual?"

"Yes, please," they answer in unison.

"What about you, Jo?" Cain looks at me. "What can I get ya?"

"I'll have a beer, whatever you have on tap."

Cain raps his knuckles on top of the table. "Comin' right up."

"So, Promise tells us you're a nurse." London directs the question toward me.

I nod. "Yes. I work in the ER over at Hopedale. My daughter and I just moved here from Tennessee."

"That's cool. Do you have family back in Tennessee?" Ruby asks.

I respond to this question the same way anytime it's asked. "I do. My aunts, Maggie and June. I had been living with them since I was eighteen. They've been helping me raise my daughter the past fifteen years." I purposely don't include my parents in any conversation about family. To me, they stopped being my family when I was eighteen.

Steering the conversation away from me, I ask, "What about y'all? I already know Promise is a lawyer, and Sadie owns a salon. But what about you two?" I look to London and Ruby.

"Actually, I'm also a lawyer," London tells me. "I own a practice with Promise."

"That's great." I beam. "What about you, Ruby?"

"I'm a teacher. I teach kindergarten," she supplies.

"Oh, wow. That must be fun and challenging." I laugh.

"It's definitely interesting. I love kids, though." Ruby grins.

We're interrupted when Cain returns with our drinks. "Here ya go, ladies." Cain places our drinks down on the table.

"Is Fender playing tonight?" Promise asks. "I was hoping Jo would get to hear him."

"Yep. He's about to go on." Cain looks over his shoulder, and we all follow his line of sight. "Here he is now."

Shit! What the hell. Dread forms in the pit of my stomach at the sight of Sawyer making his way toward us. And I know the second he sees me because the easy-going expression he had moments ago vanishes and is replaced with red hot anger. And before I have a chance to flee, Promise waves him over.

"Hey, Fender. Come over here. I want you to meet..."

Promise doesn't get a chance to finish her sentence before Sawyer's presence looms over me. "What the fuck are you doin' here?" he spits.

"The fuck, brother?" Cain turns to Sawyer.

As for Promise and her friends, they all just stare at him with their mouths open in shock.

Completely ignoring Cain and the shocked expressions from everyone else, Sawyer continues, "I asked you a damn question, Jo. What the fuck are you doin' here? You followin' me or some shit?"

The air in the room crackles, and the tension between Sawyer and me is suffocating. I have an overwhelming need to flee, but my entire body has gone numb. My lack of response sets Sawyer off even more.

"Answer me!" he bellows, bringing his fist down on the table in front of me, making the glasses rattle. I flinch at the raw anger rolling off him in waves.

"Okay, what is going on?" Promise's gaze ping pongs back and forth between Sawyer and me. "Do you two know each other?"

At her question, I manage to find my voice. "No," I say in a whisper, but Sawyer hears me.

His face scrunches with disdain. "No? Are you really going to fuckin' sit there and say you don't know me? That's rich."

On shaky legs, I stand. "I don't know you." I avoid looking at him when I say this. "The Sawyer Huntington I knew would have never spoken to me as you did."

The chuckle that slips past Sawyer's lips is so menacing, it makes my skin crawl. "Yeah, well, the Jo I used to know wouldn't have spread her legs for me then a few days later, tied herself to another man."

There are audible gasps from Promise and her friends as Sawyer spits his venomous insults my way, and without thinking I launch myself in his direction, and my palm lands across his cheek with a loud crack. "You don't know anything," I choke out.

"I know all I need to know when it comes to you," Sawyer counters.

Out of the corner of my eye, I see Promise look at Sawyer, then at me, then back to Sawyer, as if we are a puzzle piece. Then something flashes across her face, and her eyes widen. I ignore her reaction and whatever it is she thinks she knows. Instead, I keep my focus on the man in front of me.

Twisting, I snatch my purse from the table then turn back to the one man who ripped my heart out when I was eighteen and who's held it ever since. "You, Sawyer Huntington, are as clueless today as you were fifteen years ago." Giving him my back, I storm out of the bar. By some miracle, I manage not to break down until I'm tucked away safely in my car. But the moment I slam the door shut, tears start flowing down my face. And they don't stop until I turn on the block to my house. There is no way I can go home a mess and my daughter not ask questions. Questions I'm either not prepared to answer, or I don't have the answer to. Hell, by Sawyer's remarks back at the bar, I have my own questions. I was stunned at his wild accusation. It felt like someone stabbed me in the heart.

Parking in the driveway, I dig some tissue out of the glovebox and wipe away the mascara running down my face. Before climbing out of the car, I take a few deep cleansing breaths to try and calm my nerves.

I climb out of my car. The loud roar of a motorcycle engine barrels down the street, and a moment later Sawyer is pulling up the driveway. I watch in panic as he cuts the engine and climbs off his bike. He can't be here.

"You need to leave," I tell him.

"No," is his one-word answer.

"Yes. Leave right now." I point to his bike.

Sawyer stands firm and crosses his arms over his broad chest. If I didn't hate him so much, I would admire how good he looks. Sawyer, at eighteen, was handsome, but as a grown man with all those muscles and that beard, he's down-right beautiful.

"I'm not leavin' until you answer my damn question. What are you doing in New Orleans, and what were you doing at Twisted Throttle?"

"You have no right to ask me anything about my life. Now leave."

Sawyer ignores my demand. "New Orleans is my town, and I damn well have every right askin' why you're here."

Closing the distance between us, I step right up in Sawyer's face and seethe, "Go to hell." I go to turn away, only to have his hand clamp down around my bicep, pulling me back. "Answer the goddamn question, Jo." His nostrils flare.

"Kiss my ass, Sawyer. I wanted to talk yesterday, and you were a jerk. So, guess what, you lost your chance." I jerk my arm free from his grip. "Now, leave. I won't ask you again."

Sawyer goes to open his mouth, but something over my shoulder catches his attention. I peer back, and that's when I see my daughter's shadow in the house's front window as she peeks through the curtain.

"Who the fuck you got in there?" Sawyer growls.

My head whips back around. "Again, that is none of your business," I say through clenched teeth.

"I want answers," he grits back.

"Well." I wrench my arm out of his hold. "We don't always get what we want."

Sawyer goes to speak again, but I continue. "I wanted the boy I fell in love with years ago to not disappear and leave me with nothing but broken dreams and a shattered heart. I didn't want to spend the past fifteen years with my own unanswered questions. I never wanted to move to a new town and have my life turned upside down because you're here."

I witness several emotions play out on Sawyer's face as each word falls from my mouth. Anger, hurt, confusion. But I don't have it in me to stand here and pick apart all the emotions swirling around us.

On wobbly legs, I start to back away. Sawyer reaches out to grab me again but pauses when he sees me flinch. "You have ten seconds to get back on your bike and leave, or I'm calling the police."

His body jerks at my threat.

"I would never hurt you. No matter how pissed I am."

I see Sawyer's gaze flick down to my arm, and he notices I'm rubbing over the spot where he grabbed me. Wait, does he think that's why I threatened to call the cops? Because he grabbed me? I'm not rubbing the spot because he hurt me. It's because his touch feels like it was going to burn a hole through my body. It's because having his hands on me in any way brings back so many memories. I don't tell him that. Instead, I do the asshole thing.

"Ten seconds, Sawyer." With those parting words, I turn and head up the driveway to the front door of the house. It takes all the strength I can muster not to look back, and I breathe a sigh of relief when I hear his motorcycle engine start up.

"Mom, who was that man?" As expected, my daughter is on me as soon as I step through the front door.

I look around her into the living room. "Where is Maddy?"

"In the bathroom." Sawyer follows me down the hall to my bedroom. "Mom."

"He's just a guy from the bar. I accidentally left my purse, and he was kind enough to bring it to me."

"You left your purse?" Sawyer gives me a skeptical look. "That's not like you."

"Right?" I do my best to make light of my lie. "Thank goodness that man was kind enough to return it."

"He looked mean. It was like he was mad at you for something."

Sitting at the foot of my bed, I start taking off my heels. "Hmm. I didn't notice." I peer up at my daughter and give her a fake smile. "I'm serious, Ladybug. He was just some guy who was kind enough to bring me my purse. Nothing more."

"You sure? You seem kind of off." I note the worried tone in my daughter's voice.

Standing, I pull her in for a hug. "I'm good. I promise. Now, go back to your friend."

It's not until Sawyer goes back to her friend I'm safe behind my closed bedroom door that I allow myself to break down.

9

FENDER

It's a struggle getting out of bed this morning. "Fuck," I groan the moment the sunlight punches me in the face when I crack open my eyes. I rub my temples, trying to relieve the pressure. I feel like roadkill, and my head is throbbing. While reaching for my phone to check the time, my hand knocks against an empty bottle of whiskey. Then events from last night become a heavy reminder as to why I'm hungover. Why now? After all this time and of all the places she could have gone, why did Jo have to pick New Orleans? I move slowly across the room, step into the bathroom and splash cold water on my face, then stare at my reflection in the mirror. I'm dressed in yesterday's clothes. It's been a while since I drank so much I passed out. I don't even remember getting home last night. My only recollection is deciding to follow Jo home. Why? Because I wanted answers. Because I wanted to know why she acted like she's the one who was done wrong. Like I'm the one who hurt her. Except I left with nothing but more questions. Afterward, I returned to Twisted Throttle and drank my worries away.

Between the dark circles beneath my bloodshot eyes, I look as shitty as I feel. I slowly strip the clothes from my body, careful not to pull at the stitches on my side, and step into the shower, turning the cold water on. It's a shock to the system, but I needed to jumpstart the day.

After a quick shower, I dress, grab my phone and cut, then walk out of the room and head downstairs. I stop at my mom's room before heading for the kitchen. I lightly knock my knuckles against the door. "Mom?" I get no answer. For a split second, my stomach tightens. I push her partially opened door open more, and she's not there; then allow myself to breathe again. I hate being on the cliff, teetering with the fact my mom is dying. Any day she can take a turn for the worst. It's not a moment of *if* it will happen, but when. It's the not knowing that keeps screaming all the damn time internally.

I continue to the kitchen, where I can see my mom sitting outside with a cup of tea in one hand and a joint dangling between two fingers in her other. Strolling toward the coffeemaker, I notice Mom already brewed a pot for me. "You're the best, Mom," I whisper to myself and grab a mug from the cabinet, fill it then head outside.

Mom sips her tea as I plop down in the chair beside her. "You look like shit, sweetie." She takes a toke from the joint.

"Love ya too, Mom." There's a beat of silence between us. "Who brought me home?"

"Everest." Mom takes another pull off the joint, then carefully snubs it out, saving the rest for later. "You could hardly stand on your own. He helped you up the stairs to your room, then was sweet enough to sit with me and chat a few minutes before crashing on the living room sofa."

"Everest still here?"

"He's sound asleep." Mom lets out a sigh. "I wanted to check on you, but I just didn't have the strength to climb the stairs."

"Shit." I run my fingers through my hair, frustrated at myself. "Mom, I'm sorry."

"Want to tell me what's bothering you, Sawyer? Does it have anything to do with the club? I know you can't say much, but I am your mother and worry about you."

I tilt my head back, letting it fall hard against the wooden back of the Adirondack chair. The jolt makes my head pound. I deserve the pain—welcome it even for losing control last night. "It has nothing to do with the club and everything to do with Josephine." Images of her face flash behind my closed eyes.

"Jo?"

"Yeah." I open my eyes.

"You heard from Jo?" Her voice sounds hopeful, and she twists a bit in her chair to face me. Mom always adored Jo.

I turn my head and look at my mom. "I ran into her at the hospital a couple of days ago."

"The hospital? What—wait." She cocks her head to the right, and her hand goes to her hip. The universal mom sign for *you are in trouble*. It doesn't matter how old I get. That stare will always state she means to get to the bottom of the matter.

"I'm fine. Promise. It was just a few stitches. No big deal." The moment the last phrase exits my mouth, I know I shouldn't have said it.

"And you forgot to tell me? Let me see," she demands. I switch my coffee mug from my right hand to the left, then lift the side of my shirt up.

"That's not no big deal, Sawyer."

"I'm good, Mom—swear." I lower the hem back down.

"Okay, okay. I get it. None of my business." She sighs. "You're my only child, Sawyer. Don't go and get yourself killed before I have the chance to die."

"Mom." I give her a look. She knows I hate her morbid sense of humor on the matter.

"Anyway. Back to Jo."

"She was the emergency room nurse who helped treat me the

other day," I explain.

"Jo, a nurse?" Mom smiles. "She always did love helping people." I can see the wheels turning in my mom's head. "All this time, and she finds her way to New Orleans." I stare off in the distance noticing the leaves on the oak trees beginning to change colors. "It must have been hard on the two of you running into each other that way. So, for the past couple of days, you've simmered with this reunion of sorts, and last night's bender is the result?"

"She showed up at the bar last night with Promise and the other women." I feel the tension build in my neck, and my muscles tighten.

"Oh." Mom drags the word while nodding. "I'm taking a guess that you decided to say something to her and possibly made an ass of yourself."

Why the hell is she always right? "I may have followed her home, then demanded to know why she's here."

"As if Jo being here couldn't possibly be for any other reason but you, right? Like she knew you'd be in New Orleans? Like after you cut her off over fifteen years ago, she would magically know where you are?" Mom stares at me, her brow raised.

Damn. There she goes, doing it again. I've got nothing to say. Truth is, I was thinking of myself. After all, don't I have the right? I huff. "Aren't you supposed to be on my side?" I down my coffee.

"Honey, I am, but I also know how much she broke you all those years ago. And the fact you two left things unresolved is the perfect recipe for emotions to take control of one's action, which can lead to more heartache."

"You can't break what's already broken." I feel the coldness of my words sink into my bones.

"Sweetheart." Mom places her hand on my forearm. "Don't sabotage your future and the chance of finding love, no matter who that ends up being with, by staying stuck in the past.

Heartbreak happens. It's a part of life, baby. In some capacity, under many different circumstances, including love, we will be touched by its pain. Don't let the bitterness become the breath in your lungs. Don't let it stop you from the wonders you are still left to experience. It's no way to live. You both deserve to heal." I lock eyes with my mom. The unshed tears pooling in her eyes damn near make me come undone. Her emotion is raw because she speaks from experience. "Forgiveness doesn't release those from the wrong they've done. Doing so sets you free. You'll never know how strong your heart is until you forgive the one who broke it."

Her words hit hard.

Mom settles against the back of her seat and pulls her cardigan closed when a gust of wind swirls at our feet. A much-needed silence falls, and I stare up at the clouds drifting across the blue sky. My mom is right. I stand. "I'm going to wake Everest and have him stay a bit longer, just until I get back. Are you ready to go inside? I can cook you some breakfast before I leave."

Mom gives me a knowing smile, then sips her tea. She inhales deeply. "It smells like it's going to rain soon. I think I'll sit out here a bit longer. And you go on ahead. Everest will cook something for me."

I lean down and kiss the top of her head. "Thanks for the talk."

"I love you, son."

"Love you too, Mom." I turn toward the house and walk away.

FORTY MINUTES LATER, I'M ROLLING UP TO JO'S HOUSE, IN A SHITTY subdivision about thirty minutes from the hospital. As I'm swinging my leg over the bike, I hear the front door slam and look over to see Jo standing on the porch. She's barefoot, wearing ripped jeans and a purple off-the-shoulder shirt with her hair piled atop her head in a messy bun. I don't think she's ever looked sexier or as pissed. She crosses her arms beneath her breasts as I approach, causing them to jiggle. I take notice that she's braless and quickly returns my attention to her angry face.

"What are you doing here, Sawyer? I thought I made myself clear last night that you're not welcome." Jo taps her toes against the wood surface.

"We need to talk."

"I'm not sure you can do that without being a complete ass." Jo cocks her head to one side.

"I won't be a dick, Jo. Promise." I shove my hands in the front pockets of my jeans.

"At least you're calling me Jo," she says dryly. There's a pause of awkward silence between us, and I feel like a dumbass not knowing how to move the conversation forward.

"Sawyer," she begins but I cut her off.

"Are you going to invite me in?"

"No, Sawyer. I think it's best we talk out here."

I admit her rejection stings. "Fair enough." Jo blinks her amber eyes at me, waiting for the words to spill. "Truth is, I don't know how to look at you without feeling hatred." She flinches at my harsh statement. "It's been eating at my soul for over fifteen years." I lock eyes with Jo—my past and reveal a piece of me I've kept dormant for too long. "We were supposed to leave our small town, get married, chase our dreams—together."

"I wanted all of those things too, Sawyer." Jo reaches out to me, but I back away. I'm afraid her touch will be my undoing. Jo has always been my one weakness—always. I can't begin to forgive if I don't get the words, the pain, off my soul. The look of rejection on her face feels like a knife to the chest, but I push forward.

"No, Jo. You tossed all those dreams—us away the moment you let another man put his mouth on yours." I do my best to keep my emotions in check and my voice calm. My goal is for us to purge the past. I don't want us to hurt one another any more than we already are but fail. "Jo, you were my everything." As I say those words, I can't help but feel she always will be. "And you ripped my God damn heart from my chest. Seeing you kiss another man gutted me, Jo!" The skies above rumble, then let loose a pouring rain. Jo's eyes are red, pooling with tears that spill down her cheeks. Instinctively, I want to reach out and wipe them away but stop myself. My hand falls to my side. I wait for Jo, to see what she has to say. Her lips part but the sound of air brakes diverts her attention, and I turn my head to what she's focused on. A school bus is stopped at the end of Jo's driveway, and a young teenage girl with a long brunette ponytail covers her head with a schoolbook and runs towards us. She jogs up the steps.

"Hey, Mom," she says, looking at Jo.

Mom?

The girl looks between Jo and me, her hazel eyes appraising me for a second. "Who is this?" she asks, then glances at Jo again.

"Go inside," Jo orders, and her daughter peels her eyes off me, looking back at her mom.

"Mom, what's going on? Why are you crying?"

"Sawyer, just go inside," Jo insists.

The solid flooring beneath my feet is suddenly ripped away. *Sawyer?* I can't stop staring at her daughter, feeling like I'm looking at myself and a younger Jo.

Her daughter is initially reluctant, but she listens and goes inside the house, not before giving me one last once-over. I can feel Jo's eyes on me, but I can't seem to pry mine off the front door the teenage girl just disappeared behind.

"Sawyer," Jo calls my name, then I feel her fingertips brush along the skin of my forearm. "Sawyer."

"How old is she, Jo?" I swallow hard, feeling the lump bobbing in my throat.

"Let me," she begins, but I interrupt.

"How old?" I bark. I don't have to look at her to know the answer, but I need to hear it, nonetheless.

"Fifteen."

The final puzzle piece falls into place. I just stared into the face of my daughter today. A daughter I never knew existed until now. "She's mine?"

"Yes."

"Does she know I exist?"

"Sawyer."

I hang my head to gather myself, then look back at Jo. "Jesus fuckin' Christ," I bite out.

"Sawyer," Jo's voice quivers.

"How could you keep something like this from me?" I turn my hardened gaze to Jo and suddenly my anger is back.

"If you will let me explain."

"I want to meet my daughter, Jo," I grind out.

"I would like that, but I need to talk with her first. I won't overwhelm her like that. I want the choice to be hers."

Though her words feel like an elephant crushing my chest, I understand. And as much as I feel like exploding right now, I keep myself in check. At least until I give Jo a chance to explain. She just better have a damn good excuse. "Give me your phone." I hold out my hand, and Jo has that questioning look in her eyes. "So you'll have my number." She reaches into her back pocket and passes her phone to me. After my number is programmed, I give it back. "You gave her my name." I can't help but smile a little. It's the first genuine happiness I've felt in weeks.

"Her full name is Sawyer Genevieve Gates," she says, and I'm at a loss for words. She gave our daughter my mother's name. Jo has no idea how much that means to me. "I always loved your mom, Sawyer. She was more of a mother to me than mine ever was."

Before the conversation steers in the direction of my mom, I rub the back of my neck. "I need to go. Call me after you talk to her."

Jo twists the phone in her hands. "I will."

As hard as it is, I walk away. Starting my bike, I drive away with rain pelting at my back. The drive home feels longer than usual. I went to see Jo today in hopes of finding peace with our past. Instead, I left with the hope of having the opportunity for a different future. I've got years to make up for. I only hope my daughter is willing to give me a chance I was never given.

I don't know how I feel about Jo keeping her from me. I want to feel anger. Actually, I do. But the question is, why would she keep her from me?

Regardless of her choice that night, Jo isn't cruel or heartless.

For now, I'll focus on the possibilities moving forward.

Before going home, I decide to stop at the clubhouse. I need a beer and to calm my fucking nerves. When I pull up to the compound, I spot Riggs, Nova, Wick, and Kiwi's bikes parked out front, along with Catcher's truck. My brothers usually stop off here before heading home themselves after a day's work.

"Brother." Wick gives me a chin lift when I walk through the door. Instead of greeting him back, I stomp over to the bar and take a seat on one of the stools.

"Beer?" Catcher asks.

I give him a curt nod. When he sets the cold bottle down on the bar in front of me, I snatch it up, tilt my head back, and down half its contents.

Riggs, noticing my mood, sidles up to the bar beside me. "Want to talk about it? Is it your Ma?"

I down the rest of my beer and slam the bottle down. "No."

"No, you don't want to talk about it, or no, it's not your Ma?"

Pulling a cigarette from the inside of my cut, I light it, toss my Zippo onto the bar and take a long drag. "I have a kid."

The energy in the room shifts at my confession.

"Come again?" Riggs asks.

I take another drag. "Yep. A daughter. She's fifteen. Her name is Sawyer."

"Fuck, man." Wick comes up behind me while Nova and Kiwi join us at the bar.

"Jo?" Nova questions.

"Yeah. Just came from her place." I nod.

"What, and she just springs it on you out of nowhere?" This coming from Kiwi.

"Not exactly. Fuck." I scrub my palm down my face. "I was there when the kid was getting off the school bus. Jo was just as freaked as I was. She definitely didn't plan on tellin' me like that."

"Do you think she was going to tell you at all?" Nova asks.

I don't hesitate to answer. "Yes. I haven't seen Jo in years, but she's not like that. I think she planned on telling me but was waiting for the right time."

"How'd the kid take the news?"

I turn to Riggs. "She doesn't know yet. She knew something was up when she saw me, but Jo insisted I leave so she can talk to Sawyer. She wants to make sure our daughter is okay with everything. And I get it. I'm just some random stranger. I know she could be scared to meet me. Shit, Prez, what if my own kid doesn't want anything to do with me?"

Riggs clasps my shoulder. "Not possible, brother. You're one of the best men I know, and I have no doubt you'll be a great father. Trust me; she'll want to meet you."

FINALLY HOME, I PARK THE BIKE IN THE SHOP AND JOG MY ALREADY soaked ass toward the house. I find Everest inside, sitting on the sofa, and my mom reclined back in the chair. "We just started watching Die Hard," Mom says, pointing at the TV. "You know I love me some Bruce Willis." She eyes my dripping wet clothes. "Aside from getting caught in the storm, how was your visit?"

"I have a fifteen-year-old daughter," I say, leaving both my mom and Everest with shocked faces.

10

JO

I count to ten and get a handle on my emotions before going into the house where I have to face Sawyer and the barrage of questions she will have. Questions that I have left unanswered for fifteen years. When she was a little girl, she would ask me all the time about her dad. *Who he is, why doesn't he live with us, how come he doesn't come around?* The time has come. No more deflecting and no more hiding the truth, and my feelings toward the father of my child don't factor into this situation. Because regardless of how he has been treating me, I know Sawyer will be good to our daughter. The reality of just how drastically our lives are about to change slams into me at full force when I walk through the front door.

"Mom!" Sawyer scoots Fleetwood from her lap and jumps off the couch, barreling toward me. "What's going on? Who is that man? Did he do something to you?" Her questions are rushed.

"Ladybug." I place my hands on her shoulders. "Let's go sit down." I nod toward the kitchen table.

"You're worrying me." Sawyer starts to fidget.

"There's nothing to worry about. Now come sit." I pat the chair beside me. "Before I answer all your questions, I want you to know that everything is going to be okay."

"Mom." Sawyer grips my hand.

I take a deep breath. "When I found out I was pregnant, that was the happiest day of my life."

Sawyer smiles. "I know. You tell me that all the time."

Reaching up, I cup her cheek. "That's because I don't ever want you to forget how much I love you."

I take a minute to collect my thoughts. "Anyway, since the day you were born, it's been us against the world. We make a great team. But I know you have always wondered about who your father is. When you were younger, you didn't understand why other kids had a dad and you didn't. I used to tell you that your father was a great man, but he could just not be with you right now. It was a crappy excuse, I know. But you know I hate lying. Then as you got older, you stopped asking. I know it was wrong of me, but I was glad you did. I didn't know what the right excuse was to tell you anymore."

"I never stopped wondering," Sawyer tells me. "But I remember the look on your face the last time I asked about him. You got this sad, faraway look in your eyes." She shrugs. "I hated seeing that look of pain. So, I never brought up the subject of my dad again."

"I'm sorry, Sawyer. I'm sorry I never told you, and I'm sorry I made you feel like you couldn't come to me and ask."

"Does all this have something to do with the man that was here?"

"Yes." I nod. "The man that you saw last night, the man you saw here just now—his name is Sawyer Huntington."

My daughter looks at me with confusion for a beat. Then I watch her reactions as what I said dawns on her.

"His name is Sawyer, like mine?"

"Yes, Ladybug. Like you. Exactly like you. I named you after him, after your father."

The silence hanging between Sawyer and me is agonizing, but I have to be patient while she processes the news.

"Does...does he know?" she asks.

"Yes. He didn't before, but he does now. He knew almost the second he laid eyes on you."

"And he lives here in New Orleans?"

I nod again.

"Did you know he was here? Have you known this entire time?"

The accusation hurts, but it's also warranted.

"No. I didn't know Sawyer lived here. I haven't seen or heard from him since I was eighteen. Your father and I grew up together. His mom worked for my parents. We were friends at first, and as we got older, we became more. My father disapproved of our relationship, though."

Sawyer's expression turns sad. She knows a little about my parents. About how I left home when I was eighteen.

"Is that why my dad left? Because your dad didn't want you two to be together?"

"No." I shake my head. "My father had always been vocal about not wanting us together, but Sawyer didn't care. Neither did I. We were in love. We had plans to live together after graduation. We had it all worked out. Sawyer wanted to play music, and I wanted to be a nurse and to be free of my parents."

"So, what happened?"

I sigh. "I'm still not one hundred percent certain. That's some of what we were talking about when you came home. I have a feeling there was some misunderstanding on both our parts back then." I shake my head. "That's not for you to worry about. That's for me and Sawyer to work out."

Sawyer sighs. "This is all too much." She goes quiet. "Why did you move in with Aunt Maggie and Aunt June then?"

"After Sawyer left town and disappeared, I found out I was pregnant. When I finally worked up the nerve to tell my parents, my father lost it. He demanded I not go through with it." I grab Sawyer's hand. "That was never an option. I loved you the moment those two lines appeared on the test. I may not have been sure about a lot then, but one thing I knew without a doubt was I wanted you. That's why after my father blew up at me, I packed my bags, left, and never looked back. Best decision I ever made."

Sawyer opens her mouth to say something then stops herself.

"What is it, sweetheart?" I hedge. "You can say or ask anything."

"Did...did you try to find my dad after he left?"

Here comes the part that has me eaten up with guilt. "I did. I went to talk to his mom. She refused to tell me anything. Sawyer's mom is a wonderful lady, and she's always been kind to me, but her loyalty was with her son. I couldn't fault her for that."

"Not even when you told her you were pregnant?" Sawyer asks.

This is where one of many mistakes was made. One of the reasons I carry so much guilt. "I never told his mom I was pregnant."

"What? Why not?"

"I don't know. Thinking back on it now, there was no good reason why I didn't tell her. I guess it's because I believed Sawyer left because he didn't want to be with me anymore; he didn't love me as he said. I made a choice to let him go. To let the dreams we had planned go. Instead, I chose to get away from my parents and do whatever I had to do to make the best life for my baby." I sigh. "The truth is, I made a mistake. Yes, I was young and scared and had a broken heart, but I should have made a better choice when it came to your father." I scoot the chair closer to my daughter. "I'm sorry, Ladybug. I'm sorry that I didn't do right for you. I'm sorry that I made a terrible mistake and because of that, you had to grow up without your dad."

Sawyer squeezes my hand again. "I know you did the best you could, mom. I'm not blaming you."

"Come here." I pull her close to my chest, hugging her tight.

When I pull back, I notice she has shed a few tears, and I use the pad of my thumb to wipe them away. "How do you feel about meeting him?" I ask and carefully study her reaction.

Sawyer nibbles her bottom lip, seeming unsure. "Does he want to meet me?"

"Oh, sweetheart, he absolutely wants to meet you. He wanted to when he was here but understood I needed to talk to you and that it had to be your decision."

"Really?" Her face lights up.

"Yes, really." I smile.

"Do you...do you think he will like me?"

"Ladybug." I soften my voice. "How could he not? I promise he will adore you." I say with conviction. "Don't let the issue that your dad and I have going on between us affect your approach toward him. The Sawyer Huntington I used to know was the kindest, most loving man, and nothing that has happened between us makes me think otherwise. If I didn't think he was a good person or could be a good father to you, we wouldn't be having this conversation."

"Okay. Then yes, I want to meet him."

"All right. I'll text him and tell him to come over tonight for dinner."

"Can we make him our famous macaroni and cheese?" Sawyer perks up at the idea.

"Sure. How about I make the fried chicken, and you make the mac and cheese?"

"Okay!" Sawyer jumps up. "I love you," she says, then throws her arms around my neck.

"I love you too, Ladybug.

I can't help but laugh at her excitement. And though I'm happy for my daughter, there is still a smidge of doubt in the pit of my stomach that this whole thing can turn sour. I'd never forgive myself if Sawyer got hurt. Pushing those thoughts away, I pull my phone from my back pocket, find the number Sawyer saved in my phone, and shoot him a text.

Me: I talked to Sawyer. She wants to meet you. Dinner at 7:00?

His reply is instant.

Sawyer: I'll be there.

My stomach sinks a bit at his short response, but another text comes in a second later.

Sawyer: How did she take the news?

Me: She's great. She asked if I thought you'd like her. I told her she had nothing to worry about. Excited to see you. She's making you dinner now.

Sawyer: You're right. She has nothing to worry about. And I plan on proving it to her.

Me: See you at 7:00

When he doesn't text back, I decide to go fix dinner.

"Mom, we don't have the cheese I need to make the macaroni." Sawyer is frantically looking through the refrigerator when I look up from my phone.

"Okay, okay. Calm down. We have plenty of time to run to the store."

Sawyer's head pops up from behind the refrigerator door. "Can we bake a cake, too? Triple chocolate like Aunt Maggie makes?"

"Sure." I smile.

"Sweet!"

11

FENDER

I look at my reflection in the steamed-up mirror above the bathroom sink, my gut tight with nerves. I haven't the slightest clue on how to be a dad. I run a brush through my hair and beard, then stroll into the bedroom, where my clothes lay at the foot of the bed. It's my usual attire of jeans, a black shirt, and boots. Once I'm dressed, I shove my wallet and phone into my pockets. On the way out of the room, I snag my cut off the back of a chair sitting by the window, then shrug it over my shoulders as I head downstairs to my mom's room.

Her door is open, so I stride in. She's in her bed, resting and watching one of her favorite movies, *An Officer and a Gentleman*. "I'll be heading out as soon as Everest gets here."

"You look nervous." Mom eyes me.

I blow out a breath. "I can't remember the last time I felt so unraveled."

Mom laughs softly. "Is it because of Sawyer or Jo?" She raises her brow.

"I'm like a fish out of water with this dad stuff." I dance around her question a bit when it comes to Jo, avoiding the knowing answer clawing at my insides.

"Stop worrying. Sawyer will adore you. Just remember to give her time. As uneasy as all this is for you, I can assure you it's much harder for her," Mom says, trying to fix the quilt draped across her feet. I stroll across her room, stopping beside her bed. Reaching down, I spread the blanket out for her. Mom smooths her palms over her lap after adjusting the pillows behind her back. "Finding out I have a granddaughter is the best thing to happen in my life aside from the gift of you." Mom touches my forearm. The smile she wears hasn't left her face all day.

Ever since I burst through the front door last night, soaked to the bone from the storm, and blurted out "I have a daughter," Mom has been on cloud nine. While I've been dealing with a gamut of emotions, pacing the floors at the thought of all these years I've missed and not even knowing Jo had gotten pregnant in the first place, Mom wasn't questioning anything. All she cared to know was what I planned to do about it and when would she get to see her granddaughter?

She always loved Jo.

Mom was Jo's family housekeeper. That's how Jo and I met in the first place. I was ten when Mom first started working for the Gates family. Our home was vastly different from theirs. We lived in a small two-bedroom house on the opposite, poorer side of town, whereas Jo lived where the wealthy families did. Everything about their side of the city was flashy. Lawns green and neatly landscaped, massive homes, fancy cars, designer clothes: perfect. I was always aware of the fact we didn't have money.

The Gates soon became the main family Mom worked for. They hired her to be their employee exclusively. She worked all hours of the day and night because the Gates were always hosting parties. Because of our neighborhood, Mom didn't feel comfortable leaving me home alone whenever I wasn't in school.

I would have to tag along on those days, mostly during summer vacations when classes weren't in session. The only way I was allowed to be around was if I helped, because Jo's parents didn't want some kid underfoot. So, whenever I wasn't helping my mom, I would hang with Daryl, the maintenance man who took care of the property's upkeep. If it needed fixing, he did it. If the lawn required mowing, he did it. Soon, Jo and I became friends and started hanging out a lot. At first her parents didn't like it but then eventually they realized if Jo was busy playing with me, she was out of their hair. The Gates had money pouring out their asses. I don't remember ever seeing Jo's parents lift a finger to do a damn thing for themselves, aside from lifting a cocktail to their lips.

A Harley's engine drags my thoughts from the past, and I watch Everest as he heads in my direction. He rolls his ride into the shop. "How's it goin'?" he asks, after shutting off the engine.

"About to head out. I'm runnin' a bit behind schedule."

"I still can't wrap my head around you havin' a kid." He shakes his head. "Crazy, man."

I let go of some nervousness on a heavy exhale. "Yeah, brother. I'm still processing it myself."

"You've got this, brother." Everest climbs off his bike. "You're a good guy, and you'll learn to be a damn good dad."

I nod, hoping like hell he's right. I'm jumping in headfirst and blind as fuck. "Mom is inside watching a movie." I look at Everest, and he nods. "I appreciate all the time you spend out here. You putting your life on hold so she isn't alone when I can't be here means a fuck ton to me, brother."

"Your mom is a good woman. She reminds me a lot of my mom when she wasn't sick."

Everest lost his mom back in high school to suicide. I fucking hate it for him. No kid should have gone through the shit he did. "Not sure when I'll be in," I tell him.

"No problem. If you don't mind, I'll crash on your couch tonight."

"Sure." I start my bike, then roll out of the shop and hit the road.

A SHORT TIME LATER, AS THE SUN IS SETTING, I PULL INTO JO'S driveway. Sitting on his porch, the neighbor next door catches my eye as I get off the bike. "Hey." Jo's voice pulls my attention away from the man, and I look in her direction where she's standing just outside her front door. My eyes drift down her body and I admire the way her jeans hug her curves just right, and the bit of cleavage that her shirt exposes is enough to make me want to rediscover what else she has going on beneath her clothes. My eyes finally settle on her makeup-free face as I step onto the porch. Even after all this time, I can't help finding her attractive. I get lost counting the spattering of speckles across the bridge of her nose and apples of her cheeks. Jo is a knockout. Not one woman has ever held a candle in comparison. "I was starting to think you changed your mind."

"Never." I take a step closer to Jo and fight the urge to reach for her. The soft, warm, and sweet scent of her perfume is intoxicating. Before I realize it, I'm leaning forward, whispering in her ear like old times. "You're beautiful, Jo." The warmth of my breath grazes the surfaces of her skin, making her breath catch.

"Mom." The sound of Sawyer shouting from inside knocks me from my current state and I back away.

I clear my throat. "Sorry."

"No—it's—don't worry about it," Jo stammers.

"Mom," Sawyer shouts again, but this time her voice is closer than before. "Did I hear—" She bursts out the front door. "Oh." She stops short of stepping out all the way. "Hi." Her eyes fall on me.

"Hey," I reply.

Sawyer shuffles from foot to foot, her gaze darting back and forth between my face and her mom's. "I need help with something in the kitchen." Her eyes dart back to me.

"On my way," Jo says. Sawyer shifts her gaze to mine once more, then gives me a small smile before retreating inside the house. Jo hugs herself. "She has been a bundle of nervous energy all day."

"She isn't the only one," I admit.

"Listen, Sawyer. I'm sorry. I didn't know what to do after you left, and I found out...."

"I don't want this evening weighed down with our shit, Jo. Let's focus on tonight and get to know each other again." This time, I don't stop myself from reaching out and brushing loose strands of hair from her face, tucking them behind her ear. My fingertips brush across the flesh just below her earlobe, and the chill bumps breaking out over her arms don't go unnoticed. Neither does the look in her eyes. The same look she would get so long ago when I touched her. "Yeah?"

Jo lets out a breathy, "Yeah." Then she shifts, looking around me. I turn to see what has her attention. It's her neighbor, who stands then disappears into his house. Jo shivers. "That guy gives me the creeps."

"He botherin' you?" My body goes stiff at the thought of someone fucking with her or my daughter.

"No. There's just something about him." I look back at the guy's porch and see the blind in the front window moving. I plan then on finding out who the fuck he is. "Come on. Dinner should be ready."

When we walk into the kitchen, Sawyer puts finishing touches on the dining table. "Somethin' is smellin' good up in here." I walk over and glance at the dishes sitting on the counter. "You ladies have been busy." I sniff the air. "Is that chocolate cake I'm smellin'?"

Sawyer smiles. "Triple chocolate, with homemade buttercream icing."

"My favorite." I grin.

"Mine too." Sawyer beams. She grabs a platter of food, as does Jo. There's one left on the counter, so I help, taking it to the table.

"Anything else I can help with?" I ask.

Jo looks the table over, then glances around the kitchen. "Nope. Have a seat." She points to one of the three spots set at the table. Jo, across the kitchen, grabs a wine glass from the cabinet and a bottle of red wine sitting near the fridge. "Would you like wine or beer?"

"Beer sounds good, babe."

"Can I have some wine? Since it's a special occasion and all," Sawyer asks, taking a seat across the table from me, and I try to hold back a laugh.

Jo reaches into the refrigerator, grabbing a bottle of beer and a can of soda. "That would be a hard no." Jo shuts the door with her hip and returns to the table, her hands full. "Nice try, though." I stand, taking the beer and soda from her grasp, then pull out her chair. "I see you still make use of your manners," she observes.

"My momma raised me right." I slide the can to Sawyer, then pop the top of the beer bottle with the back of my skull pinky ring after taking my seat.

"Well, let's dig in." Jo pours her wine. Sawyer is the first to dig in and fill her plate, and I'm quick to do the same. "How is your mom these days?"

I don't know of any other way to say it. I hate even bringing it up. "Mom has cancer." I load my plate with macaroni and cheese, another favorite, and I'm inclined to believe Jo remembered the fact.

"What?" Jo pauses mid-scoop into the dish of green beans. "Sawyer." She lets loose the spoon in her hand and sets her plate down.

"We found out over a week ago there's nothing more that can be done." I hate the sadness I see when I lock eyes with Jo. "She won her first battle against breast cancer several years ago, but this time...."

"Sawyer, I'm so sorry." Sorry seems to be the only thing to say about the situation.

Sawyer looks up from her plate. "So, she's dying?"

Her words hit harder than I'd like. "Yeah, baby girl." I take a deep breath. "I told her all about you."

"You did?" Sawyer perks back up.

"She's excited and wants to meet you."

Sawyer looks at Jo. "When can I meet my grandma?"

Jo sits her glass down after taking a sip of wine. "I don't know, baby. You have school, and I have work. I'm not sure when we would have time to travel to Tennessee."

"Actually, Mom is livin' with me," I'm quick to inform them. "As a matter of fact, I'm supposed to invite you both to dinner at my place tomorrow night."

Sawyer looks at her mom, hopefully. Jo looks at me, her eyes glistening a bit with emotion. She nods. "We'd love to."

"Then it's settled." I rub my hands together. "Now, tonight isn't supposed to be sad. Mom—" I look at Sawyer. "Your grandma wouldn't have it. She isn't about sittin' around feelin' sorry for herself or anyone else. She's about livin' and laughin'—enjoying life."

"Genevieve was always a light of optimism," Jo agrees.

Silence falls for a few minutes before I speak. "So, Sawyer. Let me have it. Tell me something about you."

"Um, well..." Sawyers gives pause for a beat. "I mean, not a lot to tell. I hate spinach. Black is my favorite color. Purple is a close second. Music is life, and I will fight anyone who doesn't think Stevie Nicks isn't the greatest songstress ever." Sawyer takes a bite of her food. "Mom says you used to sing?"

"Sawyer, finish the food in your mouth before speaking," Jo fusses, but smiles at our daughter's eagerness to know.

"Sorry." My daughter downs some of her soda.

"I still do—even have a small studio at my house."

"No way!" Sawyer becomes excited. "Are we talking a bedroom with foam on the walls and a computer or like an authentic recording studio?"

I chuckle. "It's a little bigger than a bedroom and very professional with state-of-the-art equipment."

"That's so cool." Sawyer smiles, and I love the fact we share the same love for music.

"Actually, Sawyer has a beautiful singing voice." Jo gushes over our daughter for a second. "I hope you can hear her sing one day."

"Mom." Sawyer rolls her eyes. "Stop."

"What? I'm allowed to brag about my talented daughter." Jo beams.

For another hour, casual conversation between us flows. Sawyer talks about living on her aunts' farm and how her transition to living in New Orleans is going. She's a resilient kid and has a firm handle on life in general. I can tell by the way she views changes in her life how well Jo raised her. She's nothing like the family Jo came from. My daughter is amazing. I look from Sawyer to her mother. Just like Jo.

"Who's ready for cake?" Sawyer says, carrying the freshly frosted goodness to the table.

"I will never say no to dessert." When I say the words, I happen to glance at Jo, who is staring at me. My eyes lock with hers for a beat until Jo tears hers away. "You got some milk? I like to put my cake in a bowl and pour a splash of milk over it."

"You do?" Sawyer looks from me to her mom then back at me. "My friends back home, I mean in Tennessee, think I'm so weird because I eat cake the same way." My daughter retrieves two bowls, a plate, and silverware, sets them on the table, then goes to the refrigerator and grabs a half-gallon of milk. She cuts me a slice of cake and prepares it the same way I would, then serves her mom a plain piece before fixing her own.

I take the spoon in my hand. "They don't know what they're missin'." I shovel the cake with milk into my mouth.

Finished with dessert and full as a tick, I stand. "Where is the bathroom?"

Jo gathers the dishes from the table. "Through the living room, down the hall, the first door on the left."

I take my leave.

After washing my hands, I head back through the living room but pause on spotting an acoustic guitar propped against a chair sitting beside the living room window. I stroll over and pick up the mahogany guitar. I pick at the strings, then lower my ass to the seat of the chair. My fingertips strum the strings, playing the beginning chords to a George Strait song, "I Cross My Heart." Something rubs against my leg, and I look down to see a cat. It meows at me and jumps onto the window sill.

"That's Fleetwood," my daughter says softly and scratches the cat's head, "How do you play so smoothly?" Sawyer comes to stand by the window. I continue to strum.

"Years of practice." I haven't played this song in years.

"Mom loves that song."

"Does she?" I smile. I play coy, knowing this is our song.

"Yeah, I know this song by heart, thanks to her. Mom says it's the only song I would stop crying to when I was a baby." Sawyer laughs, then starts humming, which inspires me to open my mouth and sing.

The words flow effortlessly, and the melody brings back vivid memories of singing these very words to Jo when we were young and in love. Then Sawyer joins in, and my heart feels as though it will burst from my chest. Her voice is haunting, quiet, and tentative. Paired with the soft raspy quality in her vocals, she's captivating. I feel every emotive expression of every word my daughter is singing along with me.

I'm rendered speechless by the end of our impromptu duet. I stare up at my daughter, who looks just as in awe. "Baby girl, that was nothing short of amazing."

"Yeah?" Sawyer picks at the curtain while staring at her feet.

"Yeah."

Feeling eyes on me, I turn my head to find Jo standing toward the back of the living room. I can tell by the look in her eyes she was transported back in time as well. The air in the room suddenly feels thick. "I hate to end things when they seem to be going so well, but you have school tomorrow, kiddo, and I have the early shift," Jo says, moving across the room.

I stand and place the guitar on the chair, then face my daughter. "I'll see you tomorrow?" Then we both look at Jo, and she nods. "Good. I'll send you my address."

"Sounds good." Jo stands by the front door.

"I'm really happy you had dinner with us." Sawyer smiles my way.

"Me too. This dad thing, I have a lot to learn, but if you and your mom are willing to stick with me, I'm more than willing to give the role all I have and then some."

Sawyer surprises me by stepping forward and giving me a small hug, and I embrace her back. "You're off to a good start."

I look at Jo, who holds a palm to her chest. *I know, Jo. I feel it too.* Sawyer's arms release my waist, and she steps back. "This whole biker thing is pretty cool, too."

And I think I just got bonus points. "I can't wait for you to meet my brothers, and they can't wait to meet you too." I grin.

"You told your club about me?"

"Hell, yeah." My admission earns a smile from both Sawyer and Jo. "I'm damn proud I have a daughter."

"I'm going to walk your dad out. Mind putting the leftovers in the refrigerator?" Jo brushes Sawyer's long hair off her shoulder.

"Sure." My daughter then waves goodbye. "I'll see you tomorrow, Sawyer." She laughs. "That sounds so weird. Do I call you Sawyer? I'm not sure about calling you, dad. Not yet."

"Call me whatever you're comfortable with," I say, and Sawyer nods, then walks off toward the kitchen.

I open the front door and wait for Jo to step out. The night air is a little cool but comfortable. "You guys really hit it off tonight."

"Yeah. She's a great kid, Jo. You've done an outstanding job raising our baby girl."

"My aunts helped. I don't know what I would have done without them." Jo walks beside me down the porch steps over to my bike. "I really am sorry to hear about your mom. I love her, you know."

"She cares for you too."

Jo tilts her head back and looks at me. "Sawyer, I know you need answers. And I'm willing to tell you all the truths I have to tell."

"Not now, Jo."

"I just think we need to clear the air." Jo sighs heavily.

I feel resentment and bitterness boiling on the inside, but tamp it down. "It's not really about us anymore, Jo. It's about our daughter. Tonight was a good and fresh start to something. Let's not fuck it up with our past."

"You're right."

I stare down at Jo's face, getting distracted by the moonlight reflecting in her eyes. My gaze falls to her lips. I want nothing more than to kiss her. "You remember what my lips felt like against yours? Cause I do, Jo." I reach out and run the pad of my thumb across her lower lip. "I've thought about these very lips on mine often over the years. Even more so these past few days."

"I remember everything, Sawyer."

"I want to feel them again," I confess and lean in closer, bringing my lips a breath away from hers. "You feel the energy between us?"

"I feel it."

My hand slips around her slim waist, pulling her body flush to mine. My other hand threads through her long hair as I grip the back of her delicate neck. "I'm gonna kiss you now, Jo."

"Okay," she breathes, just before my mouth crashes down on hers. She tastes better than I remember. Heat radiates all over my body. A shockwave of emotions pulsates from my core outwards. I feel everything good about us. All too soon, our connection ends, and I pull back, leaving us both breathless but wanting more.

"I need to go." I press my forehead against hers.

"I know."

I back away and mount my bike. "Goodnight, Jo."

"Goodnight, Sawyer."

12

JO

It's early morning, still dark outside, as I sit at the kitchen table sipping coffee while staring down at the phone in front of me. I have three missed calls from Aunt Maggie. It's not that I'm trying to avoid talking to her. The past couple of days have been emotional, and I know talking to my aunt will add more. But today is a big day. Sawyer and I are going to her dad's house to see him and his mom. I was gutted when he told me about his mom's cancer and how doctors said there could be nothing more. I'd known Miss Huntington since I was a little girl when she came to work for my parents. I remember being jealous of her and Sawyer's relationship. As a young girl, I lay awake in bed at night and wished that she was my mom. Growing up, I never lacked anything. I had all the best money could buy, but all the material things meant nothing. What I lacked was affection. I lacked love.

I didn't have the kind of mom who read bedtime stories or the type of mom who fussed over me if I scraped my knee while riding a bike. Hell, when I was twelve and got my period for the first time, it was Miss Huntington who tended to me. It was summer, and Miss Huntington would bring Sawyer to work with her. Typically, my parents would have frowned upon the help bringing their kids around, but they always made an exception for Miss Huntington because having Sawyer around kept me out of my mother's hair. That afternoon, Sawyer and I were getting ready to go swimming. I was standing beside the pool and had just taken my shorts off when Sawyer noticed something and quickly wrapped his towel around my waist without a word. It was so embarrassing because Sawyer had witnessed the whole ordeal.

"Sawyer, what the heck are you doing?" I try to push my best friend away. Sawyer is so dang annoying sometimes. "I was going to get in the pool."

"Um...I don't think you can go swimming, Jo."

"Why the heck not?" I put my hand on my hip.

Sawyer's face starts to turn red, but I don't think it's from the sun.

He leans in and whispers, "Because you got your period, Jo."

Suddenly it's my face that feels like it's on fire.

"It's okay, Jo," Sawyer says as if it's no big deal. "I know about periods. My mom has them."

Not knowing what to do, I run into the pool house and lock myself in the bathroom. When I unwrap the towel Sawyer put around me and turn to look in the mirror, I'm horrified to see blood on the back of my yellow swimsuit. Not knowing what to do, I start crying.

Thinking about that memory always warms my heart. Though it was embarrassing, it is also one I cherish. About five minutes after I locked myself into the bathroom, Miss Huntington knocked on the door. Sawyer, knowing what I needed, had gone to get his mom. Miss Huntington had gone to the store, bought me pads, and then explained how to use them. Miss Huntington told me about how special that day was because I was now a young woman. She even made me a special lunch and my favorite cake. She somehow turned what could have been a terrible day into a day I will always look back on as one of the happiest. Sawyer's mom had managed to take my mind off the fact that I was going through something monumental while my own mother was out having lunch at the country club with her friends. I'm also willing to bet Miss Huntington had called my mom to tell her, but she didn't care enough to leave the club to come home to me.

Now, knowing that the woman who treated me with more affection than my own parents is dying, I regret even more all the years that have been wasted between Sawyer and me. All the years we could have been together had both of us not been so stupid. There's nothing I can do to fix the past, though. But I can fight like hell for my daughter's future and give her as much time with her grandmother as God allows.

PICKING UP THE PHONE, I TAP THE SCREEN AND PLACE IT TO MY EAR. I don't worry about it being too early. Both aunts are up before the sun every morning.

"Josephine." Aunt Maggie answers on the second ring and her addressing me by my full name causes a smile to tug at my lips. It's her way of letting me know she's not happy about my going so long without calling her back.

"Hi, Aunt Maggie."

"Don't you Aunt Maggie me," she fires back.

"I know, I know. But things have been kind of...uh...crazy here."

"What's going on?" Her tone goes from annoyed to concerned.

"Are you sitting down?" I ask.

"Oh, lord. Is everything okay with Sawyer?"

I'm quick to reassure, "Yeah. Sawyer is fine."

"Okaaay," Aunt Maggie draws out. "What's going on, Jo?"

I take a deep breath. "I ran into Sawyer's father the other day." I wait for a beat for my aunt's reaction.

"Oh, dear. I think I do need to sit down."

I hear some shuffling through the line before my aunt continues. "You saw her father?"

"Yes. He lives here. In New Orleans."

"My, that's quite a coincidence."

"You're telling me," I sigh.

"What happened when you saw him?"

"Let's just say things did not go well."

"I'll bet. I'm sure you gave him a verbal beatdown."

"Not exactly. More like it was the other way around. Well, the first time, not so much. It was more of a shock. Especially considering he came into the hospital to have a stab wound treated, and he was my patient. The second time I saw him was just as bad."

I spend the next few minutes giving Aunt Maggie a play-by-play of each encounter I've had with Sawyer.

"You mean to tell me that son of a bitch had the nerve to treat you like you're the dirt beneath the bottom of his shoes, when he's the one who left without letting you explain what really happened back then?" Aunt Maggie rants. I knew she would react like this. Aunt Maggie is as protective as they come. "I think Aunt June and I need to make a trip down to New Orleans." I hear her shout over the phone, "June! We're going to New Orleans!"

"Aunt Maggie, no!" I rush out. "You and Aunt June don't need to come here. I'm handling things."

"Yeah, well, you can handle things with some back-up."

"Please, Aunt Maggie. This is something I need to do on my own. I love you for wanting to have my back, but I'm not the same scared eighteen-year-old I used to be. I'm stronger now. I can handle Sawyer Huntington."

Aunt Maggie is quiet for a long moment. "I know you're strong, Jo. I didn't think you weren't. I'm proud of the woman you are today, and you are an amazing mother."

"Thank you," I choke out. "I wouldn't be who I am without you, Aunt Maggie."

"You have always been the beautiful, strong person you are, Jo. I was just there to hold your hand along the way."

"I love you, Aunt Maggie."

"I love you too, Jo. Promise me you'll keep me updated. And you better tell me if Sawyer Huntington doesn't stop being a prick. I'll come down there and give him a thing or two," she says vehemently.

I'M CONVINCED THE UNIVERSE IS TESTING ME. SAWYER AND I WERE supposed to be at her dad's house fifteen minutes ago, but, not surprisingly, my car won't start.

"I don't think cursing and hitting the steering wheel is going to work, Mom."

I narrow my gaze at my daughter, who is sitting in the passenger seat.

"It might," I grumble.

"Face it, Mom. The car finally kicked the bucket." Sawyer giggles.

"I think you're right. I was hoping it would hold out a few more weeks. I guess I should call around to some shops and get a tow." I rub my temples.

"That's okay. We can go to Dad's another day." My daughter is trying to be understanding, but I hear the disappointment in her voice.

"You know what. The car can wait. I'll just call your dad and see if he can come to get us."

"Really!" Sawyer perks up the same time my phone starts ringing.

"Speaking of." I see Sawyer's name flash across the screen. "Hello."

"Where are you?" His gruff voice fills my ear. I'd be lying if I didn't like the worry in his tone.

"My car won't start," I tell him.

"Be there in ten," is all he says before hanging up.

I smile at Sawyer. "He's on his way."

Sawyer and I are sitting on the car's trunk when Sawyer pulls up in an older Dodge. I ignore the way my tummy flutters as he climbs out wearing motorcycle boots, black jeans, and a navy-blue t-shirt that stretches tight across his chest, and over his shirt is the vest I never see him without. The vest that has the patch with his club name, Fender. The name is fitting, but he will always be Sawyer to me. That was the one thing I purposely failed to mention to my aunt during our chat this morning. The fact that Sawyer is a member of a motorcycle club. It's not something that overly concerns me, but I wasn't sure how she'd take it. I also failed to mention the kiss we shared last night.

"Hey, baby girl." Sawyer goes to his daughter as soon as he steps out of his car. I watch as she lights up at the sight of him. I wasn't surprised at all how naturally their bond formed or how quickly. Last night when Sawyer came to the house, it was a little awkward at first, but the weirdness faded rather quickly. Even now, not twenty-four hours later, I can see the adoration in Sawyer's eyes as he gazes at his daughter.

"Hi," Sawyer chirps when her dad kisses the top of her head. He then turns to me.

"Here." He hands his keys to Sawyer. "Go start her up and find some good tunes. I'm just going to look at your mom's car for a minute."

"Cool!" Sawyer takes off toward her dad's car.

"You know she's going to be bugging you to drive it soon." I smile. "She gets her license in a few weeks."

Sawyer chuckles. "I'll let her take it for a spin this weekend. She'll need practice anyway."

"She'll love that."

Striding up to me, he holds out his hand. "Keys."

For the next few minutes, I watch as he tinkers under the hood. Finally, his head pops up. "Your car is shit." He slams the hood back down.

I roll my eyes. "Yeah, I could have told you that. This is the second time in two weeks it's quit on me. The first time was on the trip from Tennessee to here."

Sawyer's jaw ticks. "You broke down on your way to New Orleans? You know how fuckin' dangerous it is for a woman and a teenage girl to travel alone and then break down?"

I narrow my eyes. "I wasn't in any danger. I called a tow and got the car fixed. I know how to take care of myself and my daughter."

"Yeah, well, it won't be happenin' again." Sawyer pulls his phone out of his pocket, taps the screen, then places it to his ear. "Hey, brother. I need a favor. Can you send someone over to Jo's to pick up her car and take it back to the garage? See if it can be salvaged. If the cost of repairs is more than what the piece of shit is worth, scrap it out for parts, then send it to the junkyard."

My mouth falls open as he discusses what to do with my car without my input. And when he hangs up the phone, I lay into him. "You had no right telling whoever that was to send my car to the dump. It's my car and the only form of transportation I got. You can call whoever is coming here back and tell them I will handle getting my car fixed," I fume.

Sawyer's nostrils flare as he takes two steps toward me, his boots coming toe to toe with my sandals. "That car is a death trap. You and my kid will not be riding around in some piece of shit car that can leave you both stranded on the side of the road on any given day. My daughter's safety comes before your pride."

The words Sawyer spit out cause me to flinch like I've been physically slapped.

Realizing the effect his words had on me, Sawyer's face softens a smidge. "Jo," I

Not wanting to hear another word from his mouth, I hold my

hand up and cut him off. "No." I walk away but stop short. Something in me can't let what he said go. "You know what, Sawyer. Pride has nothing to do with it. It's called survival and independence. Those are two words a single mother knows all too well. Because that's how we live; it's how we get by. Wanting to deal with my car on my own is not pride. It's a single mom doing whatever she has to do to get shit done with her means. And for you to insinuate that I have anything but my daughter's safety and best interest at heart is downright disrespectful and an asshole move on your part. You can feel any kind of way about the jacked-up situation between us, and you can throw your sour attitude around all day long." This time it's me who gets in his face. "But one thing you will not do is judge what kind of mother I am." Without another word, I turn and march toward his car, where our daughter is waiting.

The ride to Sawyer's house is silent. Though she doesn't say anything, our daughter can sense the tension between her dad and me. Luckily, we arrive at his house in less than fifteen minutes, and I can put some distance between us.

"Wow," Sawyer breathes when we pull up in front of the house and park. The home is a light blue, two-story cottage style with a circular driveway and a beautifully landscaped front yard, full of color. The house is big with more space than any one person could need. And the more I take it in, the more jealous I get. Not that Sawyer lives in such a place, but because this is the kind of house I can never give our daughter. Instead, we're living in a sketchy neighborhood with a creep for a neighbor.

Feeling like I'm being watched, I turn and look at Sawyer. His eyes are burning straight into me, and the expression on his face says he knows exactly what I'm thinking. It makes me wonder if he's thinking the same thing. He sure didn't have a problem telling me about his thoughts on my crappy car. And now, seeing where he lives and comparing it to where I live...I shake those thoughts away. Because what Sawyer Huntington thinks doesn't matter. I stand by my earlier statement; I'm a damn good mom, and though I can't afford the finest of things, our daughter doesn't want for anything.

Ignoring the man beside me, I push open the car door and climb out. Sawyer steps out beside me and we follow her dad up the driveway.

"Mom is around back." He jerks his chin.

Sawyer grabs my hand and conveys her nervousness by the simple gesture. I give her palm a reassuring squeeze.

"Mom likes to spend her days on the back patio, overlooking the lake," Sawyer supplies when we round the corner of the house.

The backyard is even prettier than the front. In fact, it's breathtaking. The lake is just yards away, and the sun reflecting off it gives the water a blue hue.

Peering to my right, I see a lone figure lounging on the deck, and when we come into view, the woman turns her head. I'm greeted by the warmest smile as she slowly gets to her feet.

"Jo."

I observe the woman in front of me. She's thinner and wears a scarf on her head, but that is due to hair loss caused by the cancer treatment. Her eyes are still as warm as I remember, and she is still just as beautiful as she was fifteen years ago.

"Hi, Miss. Huntington." We hug.

"Stop with the Mrs. Huntington nonsense. It's Genevieve."

I pull back, giving her a grin. "Okay."

"Look at you," she breathes. "Still gorgeous as ever." Genevieve's gaze flicks over my shoulder to Sawyer. She clutches her hand over her chest. "Oh, my."

I know her reaction is due to the fact Sawyer is the spitting image of her father.

"Hi." Sawyer gives Genevieve a shy wave.

"Genevieve, this is my daughter, your granddaughter, Sawyer," I introduce.

I watch as grandmother and granddaughter hug for the first time, and I quickly blink back the tears threatening to spill. I glance in Sawyer's direction to see he, too, is just as affected by the moment.

"HE STILL HAS FEELINGS FOR YOU."

"What," I sputter. My head whips around. I take my focus off watching Sawyer skip rocks on the lake with her dad and find Genevieve looking at me.

"I know my son, and I see it written all over his face. He's still in love with you."

My mouth gapes open at her bold statement. "You're crazy."

Genevieve chuckles. "That may be, but I'm also right."

"He doesn't." I shake my head and turn my attention back to the lake. "Sometimes, I think Sawyer can't even stand to look at me."

"He's hurt, yes. But the love is still there." Genevieve sighs. "Sawyer doesn't hate you. He hates what he lost."

I turn fully toward Genevieve. "Does he think I don't? Does he think I wasn't hurt by the fact that he chose to believe the lies my father told versus coming to me? And because we both suck at communication, my daughter had to spend fifteen years without her father?"

"What the fuck are you talkin' about?"

I jump at the sound of Sawyer's voice over my shoulder.

"Where's Sawyer?" I ask, looking past him.

"She went inside to use the bathroom. Now answer the question."

I sigh. I don't want to have this conversation in front of his mom, but... "I know what my father told you the night you saw that guy kiss me. My dad told me a couple weeks after you left town. He wouldn't stop pressing the subject of me accepting Jonathan's marriage proposal. My father had been campaigning for Jonathan and me to be a couple since I was seventeen. Jonathan was already in college. Jonathan's dad and my dad were business partners. Jonathan, of course, was a shoe-in at their company. Our parents wanted the two families to merge. What you witnessed at the party that night was my father's doing. He knew you'd be there. The part you didn't see was me slapping Jonathan for kissing me."

Sawyer's jaw ticks. "I ran into your dad that night. He said you two were engaged. That's what the kiss was about. That pussy asked, and you said yes."

"Sawyer, language," Genevieve admonishes.

I don't bother trying to hide the pain that laces my following words. "You know what kind of person my father is, yet you still chose to believe him instead of coming to me."

"I saw with my own eyes that motherfucker's mouth on yours. What the hell was I supposed to believe," he grinds out.

"Me!" I practically scream. "You were supposed to believe in me and the love I had for you, Sawyer."

"Jo," he goes to say. "Your lips were on his. How the fuck would you have felt if you caught me lockin' lips with someone else. It fuckin' gutted me!"

"I'm done talking about this right now. Our daughter will be back any second and I'm not taking the chance she'll hear any of this conversation. Today is about her. You and me, we can deal with our crap another time."

"Damn right we will," Sawyer growls.

LATER THAT NIGHT, I DECIDE THE BEST WAY TO END THIS emotionally draining day is with a glass of wine. I will admit some parts of the day were good for me. The first half with my car and

Sawyer acting like an asshole, I could have done without, but getting to see Genevieve was great. A pang of sadness washes over me when I remember our time with her is limited. On the other hand, my girl has been on cloud nine, and I couldn't be happier for her. I'm determined to crunch in as much time in between her and her grandmother as possible. Sawyer mentioned his mom has her good days and her bad. Luckily, today was a good day. We ended the visit with a promise to see each other again in a day or two. Also, when Sawyer dropped us off at home, I noticed my car was gone. He promised to be here first thing in the morning to take Sawyer to school and me to work. I'm going to have to figure out what to do about getting another car, because I have a feeling Sawyer is right; my car belongs in a junkyard.

Picking up my glass and seeing it empty, I leave my comfortable spot on the sofa and make my way into the kitchen for a refill. Noticing Sawyer is finished with her shower, I set my glass on the counter to go say goodnight before she goes to bed.

"Ladybug." I go to knock on her door, but before I get a chance to open it, I hear my daughter scream.

"Mom!"

My heart jumps in my throat at the sheer terror I detect in her voice. I push open her bedroom door. "What's going on?"

Sawyer throws herself at me, her wet hair slapping me in the face and tears running down her face. "He was watching me," she cries.

I'm confused but on high alert. "Who's watching you?"

She points toward the bedroom window. "That creepy guy from next door. I just got out of the shower and was brushing my hair before bed. I looked over, and he was watching me through the blinds. I didn't know they were open."

Gut-wrenching anger twists at my insides. That son of a bitch. "Come on." I keep my arm around my girl, who is still sobbing, and lead her to my bedroom, where I lock us in. Next, I pick up my phone where it's charging on my dresser. I find the number I'm looking for and press call. Sawyer answers on the first ring.

"Jo."

"Sawyer." My voice shakes. In fact, my whole body is shaking.

"Talk to me, Jo. What's wrong? And is that Sawyer cryin'?" he barks.

"That man...the one next door...he...." I can't even get the words out. Just thinking about it makes me sick.

"I'm on my way. What the fuck did he do, Jo?"

"He..." I swallow past the lump in my throat. "He was watching Sawyer through her bedroom window. She had just gotten out of the shower."

"That motherfucker is dead," he seethes. "I want you and Sawyer to lock yourselves in your room and don't come out until I get there."

I nod even though he can't see me. "We already are."

"Alright, baby. I'll be there soon. I'm about to make another call but stay on the line. Do not hang up."

The line goes silent and I don't miss the fact that he called me baby. Something I haven't heard in over fifteen years.

13

FENDER

"Alright baby, I'll be there soon. I'm about to make another call but stay on the line. Do not hang up." I'm behind the wheel of my car, pressing the pedal to the floor, trying like hell to get to my family. I put Jo on hold and call Riggs.

"Hey, brother."

"Prez."

"Talk to me," he says, my tone putting him on alert.

"I'm on my way to Jo's. Their sick fuck of a neighbor was peeking through my daughter's window."

"The fuck?" I hear movement in the background.

"I'm going to need backup to stop me from killin' the motherfucker." My free hand grips the steering wheel. I look down at the speedometer to see I'm pushing 100. My car can easily go faster, but I hold back, knowing I'll soon be nearing a residential area. I'm no good to Jo and Sawyer if I crash or get pulled over.

"Do they know where the fucker is now?

"No. Jo and Sawyer are huddling together in the back of the house. They have no clue where the guy is lurking now." Pure rage flows through me like I've never felt before. "I'm not sure I'll be able to control myself once I get my hands on the bastard."

"Address?" Riggs asks, and I hear a door slam, followed by heavy footsteps. I recite Jo's address to him. "I'm on my way." I hear the roar of his Harley before the call ends and immediately switch the call back to Jo.

"Jo. Baby, you still with me?"

"I'm here."

I slow my speed as the subdivision comes into view, then turn into the neighborhood. "I'm almost there, baby. You and Sawyer stay where you are. No matter what, don't come out of the house until I come in and get you."

"We won't."

When I hit the end of Jo's street, I turn the headlights off, and a few houses down I roll to a stop. "Listen to me. I'm here."

"I didn't hear you pull into the driveway." Jo sounds confused.

"He's here?" Sawyer asks her mom, and I can still hear how shaken she is by the tone of her voice.

"I think so, Ladybug." Jo speaks calmly to our daughter.

"Remember, stay put. I'm parked down the road. It's why you haven't heard me pull up. I'm hanging up now."

"Sawyer, wait," Jo blurts. "Please be careful. I don't want you to get hurt," Jo adds with concern, but my safety isn't in question here.

"Don't worry about me, Jo. Take care of our daughter and stay put." I shove the phone into my pocket and cautiously approach the side of Jo's house, opposite her creep neighbor's yard.

One thing I notice is the fact Jo's porch light is out. If she continues staying here, I'm installing motion-detecting flood lights on all corners of the home. I sweep the front porch, checking the front door and windows, making sure they're locked before moving around to the side of the house my daughter's room is on. There's no sign of the fucker. Not until I glance at the ground beneath Sawyer's window and find a half-smoked cigarette lying in the grass; next to it are a few older butts, indicating the motherfucker has stood here on more than one occasion.

My blood boils.

I'm going to kill him.

I cautiously make my way around the house into the backyard, and walk right into the motherfucker. He's stunned at first, and the cigarette dangling from his lips falls to the ground. His eyes widen, then he runs. The son of a bitch darts around me like a wild animal. I give chase, tackling the bastard before he reaches his porch steps. He lands on the ground, kicking and flailing his legs to break the hold I have on him. I stand, bringing the piece of shit up off the ground by the hair on his head. I feel the blade slice across my forearms before seeing it. The fucker has a small pocket knife gripped in his right hand. Unfazed, I bring my fist up into his gut three times and he doubles over, coughing, then I land a blow to the side of his head and he falls to his knees. I stomp on the hand he holds the knife in, grinding the bottom of my boot on it. His hold releases on the weapon, and I haul him back up to eye level. When I have him face-to-face with me, I wrap my hand around his neck. I back him up, slamming his body against his porch railing. "You've been watchin' my daughter through her window, you sick fuck." I bury my fist in his face a few times.

"You can't prove shit." He tries prying my hand from around his throat, and all I do is squeeze tighter until his face reddens.

"My daughter's word is all the proof I need to kill you, motherfucker." I deliver another blow to his face, cutting my knuckles against his now broken front teeth. Not even close to being satisfied, I wail on him some more. I feel his nose crunch, but it's not enough. Even after hearing the bastard choking on his own blood, I continue my assault on him. I tune out everything but the need to inflict as much pain as possible on the piece of shit.

"Brother." I hear Riggs' voice through the foggy rage. "He's done." I stop and toss the bloodied bastard to the ground and stare down at him. Lost in my anger, I never heard Riggs roll up. My entire body is tense. The son of a bitch deserves more pain. "Where's Jo and your daughter?"

"In the house."

"Go to them. I'll handle this." Riggs stares at the neighbor moaning on the ground. I don't say a word. Knowing Riggs has my back, I head for Jo's house and pull out my phone. She answers on the first ring.

"Sawyer."

"Let me in, baby," I say while looking at my hand covered in blood. I wipe what I can off on the leg of my jeans. The locks on the front door click, and it flies open.

"Daddy!" Sawyer slams into my chest. Her arms wrap around my waist in a tight embrace, seeking comfort.

"I got you, baby girl. I got you." I hold her while looking into the eyes of her mother. Jo's tears reflect the emotions I'm keeping bottled inside. I was ready to be a dad when I first found out about my daughter. I knew the moment we met there was nothing I wouldn't do for Sawyer. But it wasn't until this moment, where our daughter called me Daddy and embraced me, that it all really sank in that my life is meaningless without her or Jo.

Sawyer pulls back, and I look down at her tear-stained face. "Everything is okay now." I brush the hair from her face and kiss her forehead. Sawyer spots the cut on my arm.

"You're bleeding."

"It's nothin'," I say.

"Come inside and let me take a look." Jo reaches for my hand, and I let her take it in hers, leading me into the house. I close the door and lock it. "Sit." She points to a chair at the kitchen table. Walking over to the cabinet beside the fridge, Jo pulls out a first aid kit. Sawyer sits beside me while Jo looks at the cut on my arm. "What happened?"

"The bastard cut me."

Jo shakes her head and starts cleaning me up. "What is it with you and knives?" I don't have an answer, so I say nothing. "At least this one doesn't require stitches." She places ointment and a non-stick gauze wrap around my arm. Then she proceeds to assess the rest of my body, noticing the blood on my cut and shirt.

"It's not mine," I assure her.

"Jesus." Jo blows out a breath.

"Is he dead?" Sawyer gets a worried look on her face.

"No, baby girl." Then I look between her and Jo. "You're comin' home with me." It's the only thought in my head now, and I'm not budging on it. Just like I knew she would, Jo protests.

"I don't think that's a good idea."

"It's not up for debate."

Jo crosses her arms. "What about your mom? She doesn't need the added stress. Also, your daughter has school in the morning. I have work."

"I'll make sure you both get where you need to go." I stand. "And I briefly filled Mom in on what was going on, so she won't be surprised if I show up with you two in tow. Now, do you need me to help you pack?" I step into Jo's personal space. "I'm not leaving you or my daughter behind tonight." I palm her cheek. "I need to do this, Jo." Understanding, Jo agrees with a nod.

"What about Fleetwood?" Sawyer picks the cat up off the floor.

"Fleetwood goes too." As soon as I say that, Sawyer smiles.

"I'm going to pack." She and the cat leave the kitchen, and I face Jo again.

"Thank you."

"Only for the night," Jo says.

Not if I have it my way, I think to myself.

"Where's the neighbor?" Jo adds.

"He's being dealt with." I keep the details to myself. The less she knows, the better. "Rest assured you won't see the bastard again."

Jo walks away and stares out the window over the kitchen sink. "I can't believe this even happened. I knew something was off about that guy." I come up behind her and rub my palms up and down her arms. "She was so scared."

"I'll do my best to make sure she never feels that way again," I vow.

Jo turns and faces me. "I know you will."

I want to kiss Jo. No. I need to kiss her. I feel the pull but fight against it. My pride puts a halt to making a move. "Go pack. I need to get my car. It won't take but a minute for me to return." Then I step back. Jo sighs and slowly pushes off the counter and heads for her room.

There's no sight of Riggs when I step outside. Not wasting any time, I quickly retrieve my car parked a few houses down.

Not a lot of time passes before both my girls walk into the living room, Sawyer with her school bag, rolling suitcase, and Fleetwood in a pet carrier. "Ready." She smiles, eager to leave. Jo looks nervous.

I stand and take most of their bags. They follow me out the front door, and Jo locks the handle. I spot Riggs crossing the yard leaving the direction of the neighbor's house. Jo and Sawyer move to step behind me. "It's okay." Riggs stops at the porch steps. "Jo, meet Riggs. He's the president of my club."

"You ladies alright?" he asks, genuinely concerned.

"We're okay." Jo gives him an unsure smile. "It's nice to meet you."

"Same." Riggs nods then he turns his attention back on me. "Takin' the family home?" He eyes the bags and suitcase.

"Yeah."

"Good. I'll catch up with you tomorrow," Riggs says, then strolls

CRYSTAL DANIELS & SANDY ALVAREZ

to where his bike is parked. I usher Sawyer and Jo to the car, and my daughter climbs in, holding the cat carrier on her lap. "Mom, look at this car." Sawyer looks around.

"Get in." I hold the door open, and Jo settles into the passenger seat. I load the bags into the trunk, then walk around and climb in behind the wheel. I look over at Jo, but we exchange no words. Throwing the car in reverse, I back out of the driveway and head home.

The ride there is done in silence. By the time we pull up to my place, we are all tired. I unload the trunk and lead them into the house. Sawyer yawns as they follow me up the stairs. "Y'all can have my room."

"We can't take your room, Sawyer," Jo fusses after entering my bedroom.

"I have a perfectly good pull-out bed in my studio, with my own bathroom." I set their things at the foot of the bed.

"Does Walter like cats?" Sawyer pulls Fleetwood from the carrier and nuzzles him to her face.

"Your grandma used to foster shelter animals, including cats. Walter and Fleetwood will get along just fine," I say, and Sawyer sets the cat on the bed, where he proceeds to make himself at home atop my pillows. Sawyer smiles. "He likes it here already."

"It's late. I'll let y'all get settled. My home is your home. You already know your way around. If you need me, you know where I'm at."

Sawyer walks up, then hugs me for the second time tonight. "Goodnight."

"Goodnight, baby girl." I kiss the top of her head and give a glance at Jo before leaving.

I stop by Mom's room on my way to the studio. She appears to be sleeping, so I start pulling the door closed. "Sawyer?"

I push the bedroom door back open. "Yeah?"

"Are our girls okay?" She rolls to her side and stares at me.

"They're good. I brought them home."

"And that's right where they need to be." Mom closes her eyes. "Goodnight, sweetie."

"Goodnight, Mom."

A few minutes later, I'm pulling the sofa bed out and stretching a fitted sheet over the mattress when there's a knock on the studio door. "Sawyer, can I come in?" Jo says from the other side. I cross the room and open the door. Jo is standing there in one of my t-shirts with her hair piled in a messy bun on top of her head. The shirt is so big, it hangs nearly to the tops of her knees. The sight causes my dick to swell behind the zipper of my jeans. I move to the side for her to step in. "I just wanted to thank you again for tonight."

"No thanks needed. Just doin' what's right." I shake the sheet out and lay it across the bed. Jo walks over and helps by spreading the comforter out.

"Riggs seems like a nice guy."

"He is." I toss a pillow onto the bed.

"How'd you come to be with the club?" Jo sits on the arm of the sofa. "I'm still wrapping my head around the whole concept."

I walk across the room and step into the bathroom. "I wandered around for a while after leaving Nashville, playing music at the bars." I pull my blood-spattered shirt over my head. "One day, I found myself in New Orleans." I turn the sink faucet on and wash my face, neck, and hands. While drying off, I step out of the bathroom, and Jo is right where I left her. She allows herself to take me in and I don't mind her looking. "Riggs gave me a regular gig at Twisted Throttle. Over time, I became good friends with him and the other members." I toss the damp hand towel onto the back of a chair. "I liked what the club stands for. The brotherhood spoke to me, and I wanted to be a part of it."

"Are you into any criminal activities?" Jo picks at the fabric of her leggings.

"You askin' if I've done anything illegal, babe?"

She shrugs. "Yeah, I guess I am. You're becoming a part of Sawyer's life. I need to know."

I pull in a deep breath and sit on the edge of the bed close to Jo. "Look at me."

Jo lifts her face and stares at me. "I'm not gonna sit here and lie by saying I'm clean. Truth is, I've done bad shit, and I will again if need be." Jo casts her eyes downward. I lift her chin, bringing her gaze back to mine. "I need you to look at me. Being a part of the club isn't always pretty. And part of being in the club means not talkin' about club shit—with no one. So don't ever ask for details, 'cause I won't give them."

"Jesus, Sawyer," Jo sighs. "What about our daughter?"

"I would never let anything happen to our daughter. The club would never let anything happen."

"The kind of life you live is new to me. I'm not sure how to handle it," Jo admits.

"I get it. And all I'm going to ask of you is to trust me. Can you do that?"

Jo lays her hand on my knee. "Yeah, Sawyer. I can trust you."

"It's late." I stand. Jo does the same, and we walk to the door.

"Goodnight, Sawyer."

"Goodnight, Jo."

14

JO

It's late. I should be sleeping. Instead, my mind is reeling. My thoughts have been consumed by what happened tonight. Thankfully, it didn't take long for my daughter to calm down. I think being here at her father's makes her feel safe. I checked on her an hour ago and she was sound asleep. As for me, I can't shut my wandering thoughts off. If I'm not thinking about what happened tonight, I'm thinking about Sawyer and the kiss we shared. I'd be lying if I said I haven't been anxiously waiting for it to happen again. In many ways, it was as if I was transported back to when I was just a teenager and Sawyer was giving me my first kiss. His touch was so familiar. It was like coming home. The only difference is Sawyer is all man now, and he claimed my mouth like he was starving for my taste. Just lying here thinking about his lips on mine and how it felt to thread my fingers through his silky hair is causing the space between my legs to ache.

Rolling over, I pick my phone up from the bedside table to check the time. It's nearly midnight. I already know there is no sleep in sight for me. Climbing out of bed, I snag the robe next to me and slip it on over the t-shirt I'm wearing. The same shirt Sawyer gave me to sleep in, since I forgot to pack any pajamas.

Padding across the bedroom, I pull back the curtain and peer out into the darkness. The lake is like a pool of black ink with the moonlight's reflection. Off in the distance is Sawyer's shop. The lights are on, and I watch as his large, shirtless frame passes in front of the roll-up door, and a thought comes to mind.

Walking barefoot across the cool, lush grass, I make my way toward the shop. Sawyer catches sight of me just before I step through the bay door.

"What are you doing up?" he asks, wiping his grease-stained hands on a rag.

"Couldn't sleep." I shrug. I hand over one of the two beers I have.

Sawyer takes the cold bottle, puts it to his lips, tips his head back, and downs half its contents. I can't help but watch the way his Adam's apple moves when he swallows. I then let my eyes roam over the rest of his body. Gone is the lean build he had when we were kids. In its place are broad shoulders and six-pack abs. My favorite has to be the dusting of dark hair that starts at his navel and disappears into the waistband of his jeans. I don't realize I'm staring until I hear Sawyer growl. I'm knocked out of my stupor to see Sawyer's heated gaze zeroed in on my chest. I don't have to look down to know my nipples are hard and poking through the thin layer of material covering my body.

"So—" I clear my throat, my voice sounding not like my own.

Sawyer watches me with hooded eyes as he runs the pad of his thumb over his bottom lip. "You going to play it like that?"

The heat between us is stifling, and I choose to ignore it. Sawyer, however, looks like he has other plans. I know what he's asking. Instead of answering him, I stay quiet.

"Alright, baby. I'll let you have that play," he says. Then adds, "For now."

Setting the bottle down, Sawyer turns his attention back to his car. I follow him around to the open hood. The car is a 1967 Camaro. I only know this because of Sawyer's obsession with cars. He talked about them all the time growing up. I run my fingers along the side of the closed door. "She's beautiful."

Sawyer leans under the hood with a wrench. His hand works at tightening a bolt. "That she is. I bought it a year ago. She was nothing more than a shell. It's been a bitch putting her back together, but she's nearly done. She'll be purring like a kitten soon."

I hum, admiring the deep purple color, so dark it looks almost black. "Can I ask you something, Sawyer?"

He straightens. "Depends on what it is. If it's about my personal life, yes. If it's about my club, maybe."

I bite my bottom lip. I have been curious about some things about Sawyer but didn't want to cross any lines. "How can you afford all of this?" I ask, holding my arms up, gesturing to his shop, cars, and house. It's not as if Sawyer's house is huge and flashy, but it's a two-story home on the lake, with cars that I know cost a mint.

"The club owns a couple of businesses. The bar belongs to Riggs and Wick, but I get a cut from the garage and the tactical store."

I raise a brow as if to say I don't believe the garage and store pay well enough to live the way he does.

Leaning back against the tool chest, Sawyer cocks his head and runs his palm over his beard. "I write music, too."

I blink. "You write music? Are you talking about the songs you sing at the bar?" Sawyer has loved music for as long as I can remember. He wrote songs all the time when we were kids. Sawyer had dreams of being a singer.

"Yeah. Those songs are mine. But I write songs for other people, too."

"Really?" I smile.

He nods. "You ever heard 'Watching the Hours,' 'Waiting for Time,' 'Sweet Voice,' and 'Cold Secrets'?" he asks.

"Of course, I have. Those songs are sung by some of country music's biggest stars..." I pause. "Wait." I take a step forward. "Are you saying you wrote those songs?"

Sawyer shrugs like it's no big deal.

"Oh my god, Sawyer. That's... that's great." The sheepish grin Sawyer gives me melts my heart. "I never doubted you'd be anything short of amazing, Sawyer Huntington. I always believed in you."

My words cause Sawyer to go from on the edge of shy to downright primal. And in two seconds flat, he's in front of me.

"What...what are you doing," I breathe.

"Playing things my way now," he growls.

Hooking an arm around my waist, Sawyer hauls me against his chest. Completely on board with the change of events, I wrap my legs around his hips. Our lips are an inch apart, but he doesn't kiss me. Instead, he uses his other hand to slam the hood of the car down. Once it's closed, I feel my butt hit the cool metal as Sawyer sets me down. Keeping his solid body placed firmly between my spread thighs, he leans into me. I have no choice but to arch my back, making my hard nipples brush against his bare chest while he braces both palms flat on the car, caging me in. My chest rises and falls as my breathing picks up.

"I'm going to take you. If you don't want that, say it now." His gravelly voice sends shivers down my spine. I close my eyes on a moan when Sawyer runs the tip of his nose along the column of my neck until his mouth brushes over my skin, making it prickle.

"You don't want me to stop, do you, Jo?"

Biting my lip, I shake my head. Heat floods my center when Sawyer's tongue darts out and licks the sensitive spot below my ear.

"Say it," he demands. "I want to hear the words."

"Don't stop, Sawyer. Please never stop." The words get caught in my throat. And the second my plea is uttered, Sawyer grips my hips, pulling me toward him. I gasp when my pussy rubs against his jean-covered erection.

"You have no fuckin' idea how bad I've been wanting to taste you." The next couple of seconds happen so fast. Sawyer rips open my robe and quickly peels off the t-shirt I'm wearing, tossing both to the floor. I barely have time to breathe before I hear my underwear being ripped, my back hits the hood of the car, and my legs are spread wide, followed by his hot wet mouth covering my pussy.

"Oh, god," I pant.

Sawyer looks up from between my legs and smirks. I want to curse him for stopping. "Not god. There's only one name you're allowed to say when my mouth is on your pussy."

"Sawyer," I breathe. "Please."

"That's right, baby. I like begging, too. Now watch me taste this sweet pussy."

My eyes lock with his. I don't dare defy his orders in fear he'll stop again. I couldn't even if I wanted to because the image in front of me is too good. There's something so erotic about watching Sawyer part my lips with his tongue before circling it over my clit, causing me to choke on a sob. My legs begin to tremble with the need to come. Unashamed, I thrust my hips upward. Once again, Sawyer stops, making me cry out.

Sawyer *tsks*. "Such a greedy pussy."

"Sawyer, please. I need to come." I look down at him and contemplate kicking him in the throat when he chuckles.

"I know you do, baby." He straightens to his full height and starts working the button on his jeans. He pushes them down, far enough for his cock to spring free. My mouth waters at the sight of his erection: long and thick.

"That mouth is just as greedy, too, isn't it?"

I tear my gaze away from Sawyer's cock and look at his face. "Yes," I admit.

"Soon, baby. But not now. Right now, I need to be inside you." Gripping my hips, Sawyer pulls me down the hood of the car to where my ass is nearly hanging off. And without another word, he thrusts forward, filling me. The force of him entering me is so brutal, it causes my back to bow. His thick cock stretches me to the point of pain, but it's the kind of pain that feels so damn good.

"Fuckin' home," Sawyer growls, his fingers digging into my flesh with a bruising grip, and I secretly hope he leaves his mark on me. When I look in the mirror for days to come, it will remind me of this moment.

Unmoving, he stares down at me. Our eyes connect and something monumental passes between us; I know he's feeling the same thing I am. Complete. I've existed the past fifteen years with a piece of my soul missing. I no longer feel like that. Having Sawyer back in my life has made me whole again.

"Sawyer," I choke out. I don't realize I'm crying until he brushes a tear away with the pad of his thumb.

"Missed you too, baby. So fuckin' much." He pulls out then slowly pushes back in. "You with me?" He repeats the maneuver.

"Yes." My eyes roll to the back of my head, and I bite down on my lip.

"Look at me," he demands.

My eyes pop open, and I moan. "Don't stop."

Sawyer's pace quickens. "Never." He thrusts more brutally, and his pupils dilate as he watches my breasts bounce. Leaning down, he takes one of my nipples into his mouth. He licks and nips at it before he switches to the other one, giving it equal attention.

I dig my nails into his back, leaving my own marks. Sawyer releases my nipple with a hiss. "Fuck."

I wouldn't be surprised if I drew blood, but I don't care. And by the look Sawyer is giving me, he likes the pain as much as I do.

"Perfect," he says just before covering my mouth with his. Sawyer's tongue tangles with mine, drinking me in like he's desperate for my taste. His mouth is just as demanding as his cock.

Releasing the hold on my hips, Sawyer stretches both arms up to the sides of my head, palms flat on the hood, caging me in. His large body hovers over the top of mine, causing the tips of my nipples to rub against his chest with every thrust. Our bodies, slick with sweat, work together in perfect rhythm as I breathe in his scent. Too soon, my orgasm starts to build. I need the release, but at the same time, I don't want the moment to end. Being here with Sawyer feels like a dream, and I'm not ready to wake up.

"I'm not ready," I breathe, wrapping my arms around his neck.

Sawyer's pace slows as he studies my face. And like always, he knows exactly what I'm thinking. He knows the battle I'm fighting inside my head.

"Give it to me, baby." He pulls out then slowly sinks back in.

I shake my head. "No."

Sawyer kisses me. This time it's so tender, I want to cry. "Let go, beautiful."

"I can't." I squeeze my eyes shut as I fight off my release.

Gathering my hair in one fist, Sawyer holds my head between the palms of his hands. "Look at me," he demands.

My eyes pop open, and I'm greeted by flecks of brown and green.

"I'm not going anywhere."

My breath catches in my throat. "Promise?"

"I fuckin' swear on my life." Sawyer thrusts harder this time. "Now, let go."

"Sawyer!" His name spills past my lips. The second the vow leaves his mouth, I give in to the desire my body seeks and my orgasm thunders through me.

"Fuck." His fists tighten around my hair just before he buries his face into the curve of my neck, giving in to his own release.

I don't know how long we stay like this with me wrapped in Sawyer's arms and him still inside me. Neither one of us seems to be in a hurry to move. But eventually, we do.

"Let's get inside." Sawyer kisses me again before sliding out of me, and I moan at the loss of his heat against my skin. Sawyer quickly tucks himself back into his jeans, then bends down and scoops my t-shirt up off the floor. "Arms up, baby." His voice is gentle.

Lifting my arms, I let him slip the shirt over my head. Next, I watch as he picks my panties up and tucks them away in the drawer of the tool chest behind him. When he turns back toward me, I lift a brow. 'What are you doing?"

Sawyer shrugs. "Souvenir."

Shaking my head, I go to slide down off the car when Sawyer stops me by stepping between my legs. I peer up at him.

"I meant what I said." He tucks a strand of hair behind my ear then cups my cheek. "I'm not going anywhere. You and my daughter are my life now. I'll never leave either of you." He searches my eyes to see if I'm letting his words sink in. "I made the mistake of walking away once. Worst goddamn mistake of my life. One I will spend the rest of my life trying to make up for, but hear this, Jo. I won't be making the same mistake twice. You are mine, and Sawyer is mine."

Closing my eyes, I press my cheek into his palm. When I open my eyes, I see nothing but the truth shining back at me through Sawyer's. "I can't lose you again, Sawyer. I don't think I could survive it. Losing you was like someone taking the air I breathe. It was like having life sucked right out of me. If not for our daughter, I don't know where I'd be right now. I just...I can't go through that again."

Sawyer presses my face between the palms of his hands and rests his forehead against mine.

"Never, baby. You have my word."

15

FENDER

I shrug my cut over my shoulders before walking out of the bedroom. We're getting ready to head out for a get-together out at Pop's. I make my way downstairs, where, in the kitchen, Jo and Sawyer are placing cupcakes into containers. Jo then walks over to the oven and pulls out a hot dish of loaded mashed potatoes, smothered in cheese and bacon, to take with us. "Smells good." I walk up behind her and kiss her neck. I walk over to Sawyer. "Mornin', baby girl."

"Hey," she says, sounding glum.

"What's wrong?" I ask, pouring a cup of coffee.

"I'm a little nervous."

"About meeting my brothers and their families?" I sit down in the chair beside her. She shrugs her shoulders and continues transferring cupcakes from the counter into the containers.

"A little," she admits.

"Well, don't be. They already love you."

"They've never met me." Sawyer snaps the lid on. "Well, except for Riggs."

"You and your mother are mine, which makes you a part of the club family. You won't find a better bunch of men or women," I reassure her, and my words seem to help.

"Why don't you go get dressed? I'll finish up here," Jo tells Sawyer. After our daughter strolls out of the kitchen, Jo steps between my legs. "She's not used to having a large family. And I know that's my fault."

I'm quick to say, "She has us now, Jo. And that is all that matters." I palm her cheek. "We live for today."

She nods. "We live for today," she repeats.

"Mom outside?" I ask.

"Yeah. She's in a bit of pain this morning, so she's having a smoke."

"I'm going to step outside for a moment." My hand glides over Jo's ass. I press my lips to hers.

I leave Jo to her task before stepping out on the deck and walking over toward my mom. "Hey, Mom."

She looks up at me with a smile. "Hey, sweetheart."

"You sure you want to go with us today? I can call and let the guys know we can't make it."

"Nonsenses. God willing, I will not miss a single day of living. I want to be around my family. I want to hear children laughing and playing. I won't waste what is left of my life." Mom takes a deep breath, which seems to be getting harder for her to do. Then she takes a toke off the joint between her fingers, coughing a little.

"Need help going inside?" I don't press her to change her mind.

"I'll sit out here a bit longer."

"Mind if I sit with you?" I drag a chair over.

"I'd like that very much, son."

It's not long before we're pulling up to Pop's place. I park the car close to the house where my mom doesn't have to walk far. "Looks like we're the last to arrive." I turn off the engine and climb out of the car. Jo and Sawyer open their doors, get out, and make their way to my mom, whom I help from the back seat. "Would everyone stop fussing over me?" She laughs.

"Help Mom to the house while Sawyer and I unload the food." I look at Jo and give her a quick kiss on the lips.

"Genevieve." Pop, Riggs, and Nova's granddad strolls down the front porch steps, walking in our direction as Jo walks at Mom's side, giving her support. "It's good seeing you." I hear Pop greeting Mom and Sawyer, and I walk to the back of the car and open the trunk. Sawyer grabs the three containers of cupcakes she baked while I hold the two covered casserole dishes and cooler. I sit the cooler on the ground and close the trunk. After I give Sawyer a head jerk, she follows me toward the house.

"It's good to see you as well, Abraham. How have you been?" Mom lays her hand on his forearm when Pop offers his support, assisting her up the steps.

"Oh, hell, I can't complain. I woke up to another day and had my family around. That's all a man can ask for these days." He and Jo work together, giving Mom time to catch her breath after the last step. "I'm glad you could join us."

"I wouldn't miss it for the world," Mom says.

"Abraham, I'd like you to meet Jo and my daughter Sawyer." I make introductions after stepping onto the porch.

"It's wonderful to meet you both. Make yourselves comfortable. My home is your home." Abraham smiles at them, then faces my mom. "Well, I've got a rockin' chair with your name on it, right here next to me, Genevieve. Guaranteed the best seat in the house. That is if you don't mind listening to an old fool talk your ear off." He keeps the chair steady as Jo helps Mom lower onto it. "The women have you set up with a basket of blankets nearby and a portable heater right there for extra warmth should you need it." He points to the porch floor a few feet away from where Mom is sitting.

"Thank you, Abraham." Mom smiles warmly at him.

"No thanks, necessary." Pop settles in his chair beside her.

With Mom settled, I walk inside Pop's home with Sawyer in front of me and we run into Promise, Luna, and Piper hanging out in the kitchen. "Hey," Piper smiles. "You made it." She helps Sawyer by taking one of the containers she's carrying. I set what's in my hands down on the kitchen counter, alongside several other food dishes.

"Hey, Piper." Sawyer sets her cupcakes down, too. "Your outfit is amazing. Wish I could get away with wearing something like that on my date tomorrow, but Mom would kill me."

I glance at the skintight jeans and the bodysuit Piper has on. "No way in hell I'd let you walk out the house dressed like that, either," I grumble to myself. Not that it looks terrible or anything, but this is my daughter I'm talking about. I spot a plate of deviled eggs and snatch one, popping it into my mouth. I turn around to find Sawyer and Piper staring at me. "What?"

"You really don't like that I have a date tomorrow night, do you?" Sawyer smirks.

"I know what boys your age are thinkin'."

Jo walks into the kitchen. "What's with the face?" Jo looks at me.

"Dad is sour about my date with Jude tomorrow." Our daughter folds her arms across her chest. Luna, who's been opening packs of hot dogs and dumping them onto a plate, soon to be taken out and thrown on the grill, gives her full attention to the gathering of female forces.

Luna signs, "What's going on?"

Promise faces her and signs back, "Sawyer has a date, and Fender doesn't like it."

"Wait a minute," I sign as I speak, not to leave Luna out. "How did I find myself in the viper's den?" Just then, Nova waltzes in.

"Hey, brother. How's it goin'? I saw your momma out there.

Glad she could make it." He looks around at the women, then at me. "You look like you're in trouble." He chuckles.

"We somehow got into a discussion about Sawyer's date tomorrow night. And I simply mentioned I wouldn't let her out of the house wearing an outfit like Piper's. Not that you don't look great." I look at Piper. "Then I merely implied all boys have one thing on their mind," I say.

"All boys are horny dumb fucks." Nova has my back.

"Facts." I nod. "They have two heads but think with one a majority of the time."

"Oh my God." Sawyer hides her face. "Mom, help," she mumbles, and I can't help but chuckle.

Promise laughs. "You can't say that when you haven't even met the guy."

"We don't need to know the boy to make that assumption," Nova states.

"Dad." Piper rolls her eyes at my brother then looks at Sawyer. "This is just a taste of what's to come being in this family. Not only do you have your dad to deal with but now four uncles to add to your misery when it comes to having a personal life."

"Ugh," Sawyer tosses her head back.

Jo sidles up to my side and slips her hand beneath my shirt, her palm skating across my abs. She looks up at me. "We can't stop her from growing up. You'll have to trust our daughter will make good choices when it comes to boys and dating."

"It's not our daughter I don't trust."

"Why don't you go see what the guys are up to and have a drink while I finish helping in the kitchen." Jo bats her eyes.

"You tryin' to get rid of me?" I hook my finger through the belt loop of her jeans and tug her closer.

"Yep."

I grin at her. "Give me your lips, woman." I lean down and kiss her hard.

"Hell, I can't let you show off like that," Nova says. "Promise, get that sweet ass over here," he calls his woman over, and she moves toward him. Nova plants a heated kiss on her then releases her.

"I want someone to kiss me like that," I hear my daughter say.

I press my forehead against Jo's. "Jesus fuckin' Christ."

"Welcome to raising a young teenage woman," Jo whispers.

"God give me strength."

SEVERAL HOURS HAVE PASSED, AND THE SUN HAS SUNK LOW ON THE bayou. Everyone is sitting around the bonfire carrying on a conversation. After Jo and Sawyer got the opportunity to meet everyone, they blended in and got along as if they'd always been here. I'm sitting on a blanket spread out on the ground, with Jo between my legs and my back resting against a log. Jo leans back, pressing her back into my chest, and lifts a bottle of beer to her lips. "Enjoying yourself?" I run my palm up and down her arm.

"It's been a perfect day," she says. I glance across the fire, my eyes settling on my mom and daughter. Mom looks exhausted but refuses to call it a night. She stares adoringly at her granddaughter while Sawyer sits cross-legged at her feet, strumming a guitar resting in her lap. "I'm so glad they get this time together."

"Me too." I continue to watch them. Mom reaches out and strokes Sawyer's hair.

"Sawyer, I hear you can sing." Riggs directs his attention at my daughter, who then looks at me.

"Um, kind of. I'm not great at it." Sawyer suddenly turns shy.

"From what your daddy says, you outshine every voice on the radio." Riggs' hands move, signing the conversation. "Play something for us."

A round of encouragement passes around the bonfire, urging Sawyer to sing. My daughter sets her eyes on mine, and I give her a nod. *You've got this,* I tell her silently.

Sawyer takes a deep breath. I recognize the opening notes she begins to play on her guitar. I've never heard it done on an acoustic before. It's not exact. She's put her flair on it, with a slight change in notes and pace. The moment that haunting voice of hers leaves her body as she begins singing the lyrics to "My Father's Eyes," in the way only she can sing them, time stands still. Not even a cricket chirping dares interrupt the melodic spell her voice weaves. Jo's hand grips my knee, and my hand covers hers, our fingers lacing together. My woman anchors me as I listen to our daughter sing. Never in my life has my heart felt so complete. I get it now. Life is nothing without this right here.

Sawyer sings the Eric Clapton song with her eyes closed, pouring emotion into every word.

I feel it.

My only hope is to live up to everything she needs me to be.

There's a long pause in time, where silence hangs after Sawyer finishes the song. I look at my daughter, her eyes a mirror image of mine. Sawyer lays her guitar down, stands, and walks around the bonfire. I get to my feet and open my arms. My daughter buries her face in my chest and hugs me tight. I kiss the top of her head.

"I'm really glad you're in my life, Dad."

I fight like hell not to lose my shit in front of everyone, and swallow down my emotions. "Me too, baby girl." I step back and look down at Sawyer. "What do ya say we end the night singing a little Stevie Nicks, 'Crystal' together?" Sawyer's face lights up.

"That's my favorite."

"Grab your guitar," I tell her, and she rushes back to where she was seated before.

Jo stands and wraps her arms around my waist. I twist my body and take her face in the palms of my hands. "Thank you."

"For what?"

"For Sawyer. For us."

"Sawyer, I love you."

"I never stopped, Jo."

THE NEXT EVENING, I'M SITTING OUT ON THE DECK, WATCHING THE sunset with Jo. "You still brooding?" Jo asks.

"I'm not brooding."

Jo giggles. "Right." She gets up from her chair and stands in front of me. "He'll be here any minute. Be nice."

I sit forward in my seat, grip her hips, and pull her closer, putting me face to face with the sweet spot between her thighs. My fingertip traces the waistband of her joggers. "What do I get in return?" I look up at her and lean in close enough she can feel the warmth of my breath through the cotton covering what my mouth is watering for.

Her fingers thread through my hair. "You want something in return for behaving?" She raises her brow but fails to hide the mischievous glint in her eyes.

"Absolutely. I get a sweet reward if I don't make the dipshit piss himself." I pull the front of her joggers down enough to expose the top portion of her pussy. "No panties." Running the tip of my tongue through her slit, I take a taste. She gasps. "Fuck, Jo, you're sweeter than honey."

"Sawyer, someone will see," Jo whispers, but doesn't stop me from lapping at her again. "Oh god," she pants when I suck on her clit.

"Mom is resting, and our daughter is in her room getting ready. It's just you and me." My cock presses painfully against my jeans. "Sit on my lap." I pull her down, and she doesn't resist. I slide my hand down her pants, feeling how slick she is as I massage her clit. "Let's watch the sunset together. With our backs to the house, no one knows what we are doing." Jo leans back into me and spreads her legs just a little. "That's it, baby." Her thigh muscles quiver and

I know she's close. I dip two fingers inside her and rub the heel of my palm against her clit. Her pussy flutters. "Let me have it. Come for me, Jo." Jo lets out a soft moan as her walls clamp around my fingers. After the waves of her orgasm subside, I pull my hand from her pants and bring my fingers to my mouth, licking them clean. Jo watches me lustfully. "Later, you'll sit on my face and feed me some more of that sweet pussy." I grip the back of her neck and kiss her hard. She moans into my mouth.

The sound of a vehicle approaching distracts me from throwing Jo over my shoulder, hauling her ass upstairs, and burying my cock inside her. "That's probably Jude," Jo says. I sigh, knowing if it wasn't for this date, I'd be balls-deep in my woman. I help Jo off my lap, stand, and adjust myself, trying to get rid of my raging hard-on.

"Hurry up and put that monster away," Jo whispers with a bit of a smile.

"Easier said than done, woman. Sometimes he listens. Sometimes he has a mind of his own." I follow her into the house. The doorbell chimes.

"Mom!" Sawyer shouts from upstairs. "I'm not ready."

"Women rarely are," I jest, and Jo swats at me playfully.

"Stop. Why don't you let her date in, and I'll go help our daughter?" Jo swats my ass, then pecks me on the lips.

"Woman, you're playing with fire." I pull her into me, letting her feel how hard I still am. The doorbell rings again, and I growl.

"I'll make it up to you later. I promise," Jo says, then heads up the stairs.

I press my palm against my dick and try to make it go down some before opening the damn door.

I swing open the front door with irritation. A tall, dark-haired young man with the decent beginnings of a beard stands before me. I expected some scrawny-ass boy, but this guy looks like a grown man. "Who the fuck are you?"

He holds out his hand. "I'm Jude, sir."

This shithead is Jude? "You realize my daughter is fifteen?"

"Yes, sir."

"How old are you then?" I glare at him, with his hand still waiting for me to shake it.

"I'm sixteen."

"You don't look it."

"I get that a lot, sir," Jude says nervously. I eye him for a second longer before shaking his hand.

"Come on in. Sawyer isn't ready yet." I let him walk past and close the door. He waits for me to lead him into the living room.

"Nice view." Jude stares out at the lake.

I cross my arms over my chest and say nothing. Jude's attention shifts, looking past me, and I turn to see Sawyer and Jo. My daughter has her hair curled and makeup on. She reminds me of Jo on our first date. I took her to the state fair. It was also the night we shared our first kiss. My thoughts quickly shift from the past back to the present. I notice the way she's looking at Jude and then see the way he's looking at her.

"You look beautiful, Sawyer," Jude says, putting a bright smile on my daughter's face.

"Thanks," Sawyer tells him, then looks at me then at her mom before looking back at Jude. "You ready?" Jude nods and moves toward my daughter.

"Hold up." I stop him.

"Dad," Sawyer says in an annoyed tone.

"Have her home by 11:00 pm. That gives you enough time to eat and see the movie."

"Yes, sir." Jude nods, and I let him go to Sawyer. He helps my daughter with her jacket, which I appreciate, but I don't say it aloud. Just before they're out the door, I mention one more thing. "Hey, Jude." He turns his head and looks at me. "You hurt her; I'll kill ya." His eyes widen and I grin.

Jo and I watch them leave before closing the door. "You scared the shit out of that young man."

"Good. Cause I meant what I said."

I'VE DONE NOTHING BUT STARE AT THE TIME SINCE SAWYER LEFT. Maybe I'll just swing by the movie theater and check on her. I get up from the couch and make my way toward my mom's bedroom, stopping outside her door and knocking. Mom's strength is not the best these days, so Jo is helping her in and out of the shower. I don't know what I would do without her at my side helping. I could hire a full-time caregiver, but Mom is at ease with Jo. "We're in the bathroom," Jo shouts, and I walk into the room.

"I'm runnin' to town."

"You wouldn't be spying on your daughter, now, would you?" Jo steps out of the bathroom for a moment.

"Why would I go and do a thing like that?" I smirk as Jo sashays toward me.

"I know you, Sawyer." She smiles, and I wrap her in my arms and kiss the tip of her nose.

"I'll be back soon." I kiss her lips, and she doesn't question me further.

A SHORT TIME LATER, I PULL INTO THE PARKING LOT AT THE MOVIE theater. I hear the rumble of another bike while dismounting mine. Looking around, I spot Kiwi cruising by. He happens to spot me and turns into the parking lot, heading in my direction. Kiwi rolls to a stop. "Hey, brother."

"How's it goin'?"

"Not much, mate." He looks at me funny. "Since when do you go to the movies alone?" he asks.

"Sawyer is in there with her date."

Kiwi puts the kickstand down and cuts his bike off. "You're spyin'?"

"Yep." I head toward the building to purchase a ticket.

He gets off his bike. "Shit, I'm jumpin' on this ride." He jogs after me. I buy a ticket, and Kiwi does the same. Kiwi catches up to me after snagging himself a bucket of popcorn.

"Jesus," I shake my head. "I'm not here for fun."

"You can't go to the movies without buying buttered popcorn, mate." He pops some in his mouth. "I'm so doin' this if I have a daughter." Kiwi chuckles as we get odd looks from the people we pass walking down the hall. We enter the dark theater where the movie is already playing. I scan the room and spot my daughter on the far side near the second row. Luckily, we sneak our way to the top level undetected, where I see with a bird's eye. "That's her date? He's a grown-ass man," Kiwi whispers.

"He's sixteen."

"Did you ask for his ID?" I could kick myself in the ass for not thinking of that myself. I lean forward and glance down at the seats below us. So far, they're watching the movie and nothing more. "This is a good flick. Piper and I watched it the other week. It has some great jump scares." The masked killer jumps from the shadows causing several women in the audience to shriek. I look over the edge at my daughter again and watch Jude put his arm around her shoulder, and she places her hand on his knee. "Oh shit, looks like he's goin' for first base, brother."

I watch the shithead lean in and kiss my daughter. I'd like to say I don't know what came over me, but I'd be a damn liar. Like a matador waving a red cap in front of a bull, I see red. I snatch the bucket of popcorn from Kiwi's hands, hold it over the railing, and dump it onto Jude's head.

"What the—" Jude stands, brushing popcorn off himself, then looks up. I don't move. I want him to see me. His eyes land on my face. *That's right motherfucker.* Sawyer's head snaps back, and her eyes narrow to slits, cutting into me like a knife through butter.

"Daddy!" she hisses.

"Oh, shit," Kiwi chuckles. "Someone is in trouble."

Sawyer stomps toward the exit with Jude on her heels, and I'm not far behind.

"Daddy." My daughter folds her arms. "What are you doing? This is so embarrassing."

"I couldn't stop worrying about you." My eyes cut to Jude, who looks nervous as fuck. He should be after putting moves on my baby girl.

"Jude, please take me home." Sawyer stomps off.

I blow out a breath. "That did not go how I planned."

Kiwi slaps me on the back. "Well, brother. I'm out of here."

"You're ditchin' me?" We walk out of the building. I spot Jude opening the passenger door for Sawyer in the parking lot and even buckling her in.

"Good luck, mate." Kiwi grins, then starts his bike.

JUDE'S TRUCK IS HEADING DOWN THE DRIVEWAY AS I'M DRIVING toward the house. I slow to a stop, so he does the same. Jude rolls his window down. "Sir, I know you're looking out for Sawyer. I get it. I have three younger sisters at home, and I already know there's not a guy out there good enough for them. But I like Sawyer and respect her. I would never do anything to hurt her."

I cut my bike off, so I'm not shouting. "She's mine, Jude. For now, until she finds the guy who sets her soul on fire, I'm the one standing guard. Ya, feel me? And I have an entire MC behind my back ready to do the same."

"Understood, sir. And I'm asking you to give me a chance and not run me off. What if I am the one who holds that spark to her flame?"

Well, I'll be damned. "You've got balls," I tell him.

"Not balls, sir. Respect."

I nod. This time I offer him a handshake. "Even better." Jude puts his arm out the window and shakes my hand.

"I'd like to take Sawyer out again. With your permission, of course," Jude asks.

I nod. "You've got it."

"Goodnight, sir."

"Take it easy, Jude. Drive safe." I wait for him to pull away, then crank the bike back up and cruise the rest of the way down the driveway. I know what's waiting for me on the inside, so I waste no time putting the bike in the shop and facing the inevitable. "Jo," I call out as I enter the house. I lock the door, then toss my keys on the nearby table. "Jo," I shout again.

"In your mother's room," she calls out.

I find all three women in my life together on my mom's bed. All three not looking the least bit happy. "Sawyer." Mom gives me that *I'm disappointed in you* look.

"A bucket of popcorn? Really?" Jo tries giving me a stern expression but wavers, and she breaks eye contact with me.

"Mom, it's not funny." Sawyer buries her face in a pillow.

"Look," I sigh. "I shouldn't have wasted good popcorn like that." Sawyer flings her head up and blinks at me like I've grown two heads.

"Are you serious right now?" she screeches.

"But I won't apologize for checkin' up on you."

"It was humiliating." Sawyer throws her face into the pillow again. "He'll probably never want to see me again." Her voice is muffled.

"Yes, he will." I squat down in front of her.

"You don't know that."

"I gave him permission about five minutes ago."

Sawyer lifts her head and looks at me. "You did?"

"Yeah."

Sawyer pouts. "Promise no more surprise pop-ins on my dates?"

I shake my head. "I can't promise anything. But I won't dump popcorn on his head again." Sawyer looks at her grandma then at Jo, like *is he for real?*

"He's your father, sweetheart, and wants to protect you," Mom tells Sawyer, then cuts her eyes at me. "Even if he is a bit extreme." Then she looks back at her granddaughter. "But he means well. Give him time. Being a parent doesn't come with instructions, and no one has all the right answers on how to navigate raising a child. We're all winging it and praying like hell we get something right."

16

JO

I'm eight hours into a ten-hour shift at the hospital when I finally get to take the fifteen-minute break I was supposed to take thirty minutes ago. "Hey, Imani. You want soda or anything from the vending machine?" I ask while grabbing my purse from behind the counter at the nurses' station.

"Yeah, and grab me some chips while you're at it. Here." She pulls a couple of dollars from the front pocket of her scrubs and hands them over.

"You got it." I take the bills then dig through my purse for my phone to check in on Sawyer. As soon as I have it in hand, the screen lights up, revealing about a dozen missed calls, all from Aunt Maggie. Worried something is wrong, I don't waste any time calling her back. She picks up on the first ring.

"I have called you a hundred times!"

"I'm at work. I just saw. Is everything okay, Aunt Maggie? Is it Aunt June?"

"No, no. We're both okay."

My shoulders sag in relief, and I notice Imani watching on. I wave off her concern and cover the phone with my hand.

"Everything is fine. I'm taking fifteen," I tell Imani, then begin making my way down the hall toward the waiting room where the vending machines are. Once I'm out of earshot, I turn my attention back to the call. "What's going on, Aunt Maggie?"

"Shit," my aunt curses under her breath.

I pause next to the soda machine. My aunt's weird behavior now has me confused. "Aunt Maggie," I press.

"It's your dad," she blurts. And for a second, I think I misunderstood.

"I'm sorry, what?"

"He was here, Jo. Looking for you."

Suddenly my body goes numb, and I stumble over to one of the chairs in the waiting room. "Um," is all I say. I haven't seen or spoken to my father since the day I left home. Neither he nor my mother have made any attempts to see their granddaughter or me.

"Jo, sweetheart, are you still there?" Aunt Maggie calls out.

I snap out of my stupor. "Yeah, I'm still here." I take a deep breath. "What...what did he want?"

"I don't have a clue. The bastard wouldn't say. I told him to get lost. The son of a bitch thought he could puff his chest and intimidate me. That is until June got her shotgun and threatened to put a bullet in his sorry ass."

God, I love Aunt June. Aunt June is very protective of Aunt Maggie. I have no doubt in my mind she would have followed through on her threat to shoot my father.

"Anyway," my aunt continues, "I don't know what my brother is up to, but my gut says he's up to something."

I let out a heavy sigh. "I agree." I close my eyes and think for a minute. "Maybe I should go to him. See what he wants."

"You go to that man and give him even one ounce of your breath, and I will tan your hide, Josephine Gates," Aunt Maggie snips. "You don't owe him a darn thing. Whatever his deal is, it's his problem. That man does not get to show up after fifteen years and demand anything of you."

Aunt Maggie's use of my full name is a clear indication she means business. I also know that no matter how old I get, if Aunt Maggie says she's going to whoop my butt, she means just that.

"You're right. I just don't want him showing up at your house again because of me."

"Oh, don't you worry about us. I know how to handle my brother. I'm actually kind of sorry I didn't get to see June shoot him in the ass."

I can't help but burst out laughing. "I wouldn't mind seeing that myself."

Aunt Maggie and I fall silent then she continues. "I'm worried about you."

"Don't be. I'll handle my dad if he does show up. Which he probably won't."

"Well, if he does, you let me know. June and I will come down there so she can make good on her promise."

I shake my head and smile. "I will. I love you, Aunt Maggie. Tell Aunt June I said hi and that I love her too."

"I will, Jo. Give our Ladybug a hug for us, okay?"

I HANG UP WITH MY AUNT AND RESIST THE URGE TO CALL SAWYER, but my problems with my father are not something I should be bothering him with. He already has the weight of the world on his shoulders with his mom being sick. And though my father suddenly showing up after all these years is causing a ball of stress to form in the pit of my stomach, I refuse to add to Sawyer's already full plate. Something that kills me is having to see the pain in his eyes every day. He's slowly losing his mom, and there's nothing I can do to take that pain away. I think Sawyer having his daughter around is helping. I have loved every second of watching the bond between them get stronger. My girl is blossoming under her father's adoration, and Sawyer has fallen into the role of being her father beautifully.

"Excuse me."

My thoughts are interrupted when I hear a woman's voice. I turn to the lady standing beside me. "Yes?"

"I was hoping you could help me. My name is Stacy. I got a call saying my husband was brought in. His boss said there was an accident on the construction site he was working at, and he was injured. His name is Daren."

I recognize the name of the man. He was a patient of mine. "Of course. My name is Jo, and I was your husband's nurse when he was first brought in."

"Is...is he okay?" Stacy's voice shakes.

I'm quick to reassure her. "Oh, my goodness, yes. I'm sorry, I should have mentioned that first. Your husband is going to be fine. As you said, there was an accident. I don't know the details, but your husband suffered a broken arm. He's getting a cast put on now. I can take you to him if you like."

The woman visibly relaxes. "Yes. Thank you."

THE NEXT COUPLE HOURS OF MY SHIFT PASS QUICKLY, AND I AM thankful I have tomorrow off.

"Good night, Jo," Imani calls out as she walks across the parking lot toward her own car.

"Night." I wave over my shoulder the same time my phone rings. Pulling it from the front pocket of my scrubs, I see Sawyer's name flash across the screen and I smile. "Hey you," I answer.

"Hey, baby," he greets, his voice making my tummy flutter. "You off?"

"Yeah. I'm walking out now."

"How was your day?" he asks.

"Long," I breathe.

Sawyer chuckles. "That bad?"

"Meh. Typical day. What about you? How was your day?"

"Good. I'm hangin' with Sawyer and Mom. I was just about to throw some burgers on the grill and wanted to get your ETA."

"Mmm, burgers sound good. I'll be home in about fifteen minutes. Do you want me to pick up anything from the store? How about some beer?"

"Nope. I got that covered. I even picked up some wine for you. Sawyer pointed out your favorite kind when she went with me to the store earlier. All you have to do is bring that gorgeous ass of yours home."

"That I can do."

"Drive safe, baby."

I continue to make my way toward my car. Or should I say Sawyer's car. Yesterday Sawyer handed me the keys to the Camaro he's been working on. He said there was no sense in me trying to find another car when he has one I can drive. I wanted to argue with him at first but in the end, I accepted the Camaro. I'd be a fool not to.

I'm smiling from ear to ear like a loon by the time I reach my vehicle. I start to respond to Sawyer, but my words are cut off when a voice I haven't heard in years calls out my name.

"Josephine."

I pause with my hand over the door handle of my car. And when I turn to face the man who is responsible for so much unnecessary hurt in my life, I suck in a sharp breath. Something about my reaction puts Sawyer on high alert, because I can hear it in his tone when he asks, "Jo, baby, are you okay?"

When I don't respond and continue to stare at my dad, he asks again, "Baby, talk to me."

"Josephine," my dad repeats my name.

"Jo, who's there with you?" Sawyer's question comes out more clipped this time.

I swallow past the lump in my throat. "My father."

"Are you fuckin' shittin' me? That mother fucker is there now?"

I've always imagined what I would do or say if I ever came face-to-face with my dad again, but for some reason, the many speeches that I used to recite inside my head over the years have vanished. Instead, I am numb.

"I'm on my way to you now, baby. I'll be damned if that mother fucker gets to even breathe the same air as you," Sawyer growls into the phone. A beat later, I hear his motorcycle start up, and then the line goes dead.

Pocketing my phone, I straighten my spine and continue to stare at my father. It's been over a decade since I last saw him, but he still looks the same. His hair has a bit more gray around the temples, and he has a few more lines at the corner of his eyes, but nothing about the man has changed other than that. Right down to the three-piece suit and gold cufflinks and eight-thousand-dollar watch on his wrist.

My father goes to take a step in my direction, but he stops when I put my hand up in front of him. "Whatever you came to say, you can say from where you're standing."

"We need to talk," he tells me.

"I don't need to do anything. I haven't had anything to say to you for the past fifteen years, and I sure as hell don't have anything to say now."

My father's face turns red. "Stop being dramatic, Josephine. I'm your father. Therefore, I expect you to show me some respect."

Tossing my head back, I laugh. "You expect me to show you respect? Oh, that's rich."

"Josephine." My dad tries to chastise me like he did when I was a kid.

God, I hate the way my name sounds coming out of his mouth.

"Also," I say, cutting him off once again when he goes to open his mouth. "You don't get to show up after fifteen years and demand anything of me. I also don't have to do shit you ask. I'm not a little kid anymore. And how did you find me anyway?"

"It wasn't that hard, despite the fact that Maggie and that woman didn't help," he spits.

After all these years, he still refuses to say Aunt June's name. "You mean Aunt June."

"That woman is not your aunt."

"Aunt June is Aunt Maggie's wife, so I do believe that makes her my aunt." I shake my head in disappointment. "Not only are you an asshole, but you're also a bigot."

"You little..." My father goes to say as he advances on me but halts when we are suddenly interrupted.

"Everything okay here?"

I look to my right to see Dr. Ledger approaching. He wears a look of concern on his face as his eyes bounce between my dad and me and his smile looks forced.

"We're fine," my father answers in a strained tone. "I'm just having a chat with my daughter."

My nails dig into my palms as I clench and unclench my fists. I have no doubt my father was about to strike me before Dr. Ledger interrupted us. I have been on the receiving end of my father's palm more than a few times growing up. As I said, he doesn't like backtalk. Only this time, I was ready to give him a taste of his own medicine.

As if he knew what was about to happen, Dr. Ledger's gaze flicks down to my clenched fists and back to my dad. The fake smile he had moments ago drops. It's also the exact moment I hear a familiar sound of a rumbling engine making its way into the parking lot.

17

FENDER

Jo's father's eyes grow wider with recognition the closer I get. "You." He looks me over with a smug expression, curling his lip. "Couldn't take a hint fifteen years ago, you piece of shit?" I continue to advance on him, and he backpedals.

Jo grabs my arm. "Sawyer, he's not worth it."

"Should I call the police?" someone asks.

I look to my left and for the first time since I pulled up, notice the same E.R. doctor from my last visit standing there. "No." I answer at the same time Jo's dad says, "Yes."

The doctor ignores Jo's father and continues to regard me. "Are you two going to be good here with him?" he jerks his head toward the piece of shit in question.

"Yeah, man. I got this. Appreciate ya." I nod.

The doctor looks from me to Jo then back to me before taking his leave. I then turn my attention back to Jo's dad. I go to take a step in his direction and get a sense of satisfaction when he flinches.

Her father holds his ground, lifting his self-righteous nose in the air. "You lay a finger on me; I'll have you arrested." His judgmental eyes pass over me again. "I see you never made anything of yourself. You were never good enough to be a part of the Gates legacy." Then looks at his daughter. "What are you now, a biker's whore?"

Say what he wants about me, but I'll be damned if he disrespects Jo. I grab Jo's father by the tie around his thick neck, rear back, and slam my fist into his face. His teeth scrape against my knuckles, and I release him with a shove backward. Blood drips down the front of his crisp white shirt.

The piece of shit lifts his hand, covering his mouth. "You Neanderthal. You'll pay for that. I'll call the police."

"Go ahead." I glance down the street, knowing there's always a patrol car nearby. This is New Orleans, after all. "There's one of our city's finest right now." I grind my teeth, calling his bluff.

Richard looks down the road, then back at me. He spits blood from his mouth. "You're not worth my time." He takes a handkerchief from his pocket and wipes it at the cut on his lower lip.

"I can't handle all of this right now." Jo shakes her head. "Dad, you need to leave before things get out of hand."

"Josephine, we have business to take care of." Jo's father cuts his eyes at me, then back at Jo, and shoves some papers toward her. "Just sign."

My fists clench at my sides. "The fuck?" I knock his hand away. "She isn't signin' nothin' from you," I bark at her father, who narrows his eyes at me.

"This isn't any of your concern. It's between my daughter and me."

"If you value your life, I suggest you tuck that tail between your legs and get the fuck out of here, Richard." I give him a final warning while holding back years of pent-up anger. He stands silent and unmoving for a beat while I stare him down.

He clears his throat. "Josephine." He pulls a pen from his

pocket, along with a small business card, and writes on the back of it, then hands it to his daughter. "This is where I'm staying. For your own good, I suggest you pay me a visit." He never once takes his eyes off me. "And leave the trash at home." His worthless ass walks off toward a black sedan parked nearby, and I let him go without reaction to his parting statement. The car's driver steps out, opens the back passenger door, and waits for Jo's father to climb inside.

Jo turns to me after her father drives away. "Shit. I'm sorry about all of this."

I reach out and rub my palms up and down her arms, then tuck her into my chest. "Never apologize for that son of a bitch." I pull away slightly to look at Jo's face. "You good?"

Jo sighs. "Yeah. He caught me off guard." She shakes her head and looks down at the card she is holding. On the front are his business logo and name. Jo flips it over and scribbled on the backside is the hotel address and room number. "What makes him think I want anything from him? Or to do with him, for that matter?"

"Let me see that babe." I pull the card from between her fingers. "What exactly was he tryin' to get your Hancock on?"

Jo lifts her hands and shrugs. "I'm not sure." Jo pinches the bridge of her nose, clearly overwhelmed. "I haven't seen or talked with either of my parents in over fifteen years. I have no interest in anything that is associated with them." Jo presses her forehead against my chest and lets out a heavy breath. "I've made it this far in life without them. I sure as shit don't need them popping back up now."

I kiss the top of her head. "And don't let him make you look at how far you've come any differently." Jo pulls back and looks up at me.

"I also have you."

Leaning down, I hover my mouth above hers. "Damn right you

do." Then I crash my lips down on hers. The stress of her father's sudden interest in her and his being in my city evaporates for a moment while we lose ourselves in the kiss. Reluctantly, I pull back.

"I should just see what he wants and be done with him. I can't handle him being here."

"Not happenin'," I grunt. "What you're goin' to do is go home."

"Sawyer, I—"

I cut her off. "Not up for debate. I'm going to handle your father."

"Sawyer, please. He really isn't worth it. And the last thing we need is you going to jail."

"Babe," I place my finger beneath her chin, keeping eye contact. "Trust me?"

"Of course."

"Then go home."

Jo gazes through her long lashes at me with a mischievous twinkle in her eyes. "What do I get in return?"

She wants to play me at my own game. "You want a reward for behaving?" I raise my brow.

"That's right." Her pupils dilate.

I pull her body tight against mine, letting her feel how turned on I am at the moment, and whisper in her ear. "I want you in the worst way right now." I grip her ass. "You want me to do bad things to you, baby? You want to ride my cock? How about I taste your sweet pussy until you come? I won't stop until I've left your body trembling and wanting more." Jo's breath quickens. "I'll reward you, Jo." My hands lower on her ass until the tips of my fingers are dipping between her cheeks. "I'll claim every inch of your sexy body, baby." I drag my lips down the slope of her neck, and she moans. I smack her ass. "You're a craving I'll never satisfy."

"I need your hands on my body, Sawyer," Jo confesses, and her words make me want to fuck her right now. "That's my addiction."

"Fuck," I groan, knowing losing ourselves in each other will have to wait. I smack her ass. "Go before I have my way with you." I back away. Jo's eyes drop to my crotch, and she licks her lips. My dick throbs, thinking about her sucking me off. "Woman, you're killin' me. Go home."

Jo steps forward, places her palm over my heart, raises on her tiptoes, and presses her lips to mine. "Please be careful. Dad is not someone you underestimate." I say nothing as Jo turns, walks the few steps to her ride, gets behind the wheel, and drives away.

I hop back on my bike and head toward the clubhouse. I need some answers, and Wick is the man to find them for me.

A short time later, I walk into the clubhouse and find Wick, along with Tequila, Nova, who has Promise sitting on his lap, and Catcher, who is busy working. "Hey, brother," Catcher greets me first. Prez has been keeping him busy ever since he began prospecting for the club. He's currently building new shelves behind the bar. Catcher is a jack of all trades and has excellent carpentry skills that rival his mechanical expertise.

"How's it goin'?" I pause to admire his work. The scorched oak, stained in a rich ebony color, looks great; almost too fancy for the clubhouse.

"Can't complain. You need anything while I'm back here?" he asks.

"No, man. Thanks." I leave him to his work and stroll over to where Wick is sitting on a couch, leaned back with an arm behind his head and the other draped around Tequila's shoulders. "I need a favor."

"Alright, shoot," Wick says, giving me his attention.

I hand him Richard's business card. "Need you to dig up some information on him. Not the surface shit. I need to know if he has dirt, something I can use as leverage."

Wick takes the card and looks at it. "What's the backstory?"

"That's Jo's father. He confronted her at the hospital earlier, trying to strong-arm her into signing some papers."

"Did you get a look at the documents?" Wick changes positions, bringing himself to sit on the edge of the sofa.

"No. But my gut says it has something to do with money. That's just how that man works."

"Jo know anything about any money?"

I dig in my pocket, pull out a cigarette, and light it. "Not a damn thing. And she wants no part of him or whatever the hell he wants. Either way, his sudden presence after fifteen years of silence is more than suspicious. I want to know more."

"Sometimes, the ones you think are your family are the most toxic people," Promise says, and I couldn't agree more.

Wick looks at Tequila, who says, "Go on and play. I'm going to head upstairs and take a nap." She rubs her belly. "This kid is wearing me out." Wick stands, then helps his woman to her feet. He kisses her.

"Don't go anywhere without another brother or me."

"I know the drill, Malik." Tequila smiles around another kiss.

"You're lucky I love your sass." Wick swats her ass as she retreats.

Tequila looks back over her shoulder as she climbs the stairs and catches Wick's eyes glued to her ass. "My sass isn't the only thing you love." She puts a little extra sway in her hips.

Wick tears his attention from Tequila and looks across the room. "Hey, Catcher. Bring us a couple of cold beers and snag my laptop from the back, would ya?" I follow him to the table, where we join Nova and Promise.

"You got it." Catcher walks to the bar, quickly returning with our drinks.

Wick faces me. "Let me see what I can dig up, brother."

Two hours later, Wick closes his laptop. Turns out Jo's dear ole dad is in a financial pickle. He's full-on about to be ass-fucked by the U.S. government for tax fraud. He owes millions. On top of all that, his wife is playing dirty behind his back, taking him for everything he's got. Wick found some interesting details that I would like nothing more than to cram down Richard Gates' egotistical throat. "That's a lot of money," Promise says, still processing the dollar amount of the trust Jo's grandfather left for her. "Just thinking about how much that money would have helped her over the years, and her father keeping it a complete secret from her." Her lips thin with disgust. "I don't even know the prick, but I sure as hell want to kick him in the balls."

"Is Jo sure she doesn't want the money? I'll help her secure it." Wick looks at me. "Her father won't ever get his hands on it."

"At the moment, she wants no part of it."

"What about Sawyer? That money is probably the cleanest money that family has. Jo could easily transfer the trust into your daughter's name. A lot of good can be done with money like that. It would be a shame for it to sit there and go to waste," Nova interjects, making a valid point.

I have money, more than enough to take care of Jo and our daughter, but my brothers are right. I look at Wick. "Do it. Jo can make the final call, but for now, make sure her father can never get his hands on that money." I down what's left of my second beer, then stand. "I think it's time I pay Jo's father a little farewell visit."

"I'll join you." Wick stands.

Nova lays a kiss on Promise, then ushers her off his lap. "Stay put."

"You're so bossy." Promise rolls her eyes.

"You only complain about the fact outside the bedroom," he says, causing Promise to blush. Nova downs his beer then tosses it in a nearby trash can. "Let's ride."

"Catcher, hold the place down while we're gone," Nova shouts, and Catcher, being a man of few words, nods his reply.

. . .

THE THREE OF US STROLL INTO THE LOBBY OF A FIVE-STAR HOTEL, getting judgmental stares from a group of corporate men in expensive suits. Nothing we aren't used to. We head for the elevators and ride one up to the eighth floor, to the executive suites. I knock on the room door.

The door swings open. "What the fuck do you want?" Gates sneers, his lips thinning. I move into his space, making him stagger as I step into his room. His eyes widen when Nova and Wick step in as well, closing the door behind them. "Get out before I call security," he threatens as his attention follows my brother. Wick strolls past me. "I don't know who the hell you are but take another step, and—" Wick drags a chair across the carpeted floor.

"Sit," I shove Gates into the seat. He goes to stand, and Wick grips his shoulder from behind, keeping him in place.

"You best believe the only way you'll be leaving this hotel is in handcuffs." Gates glares at me.

I fold my arms across my chest. "Now, I don't think a man in your position would actually want any sort of attention drawn in his direction."

"What the hell are you babbling about? I have a great deal of power and many other men of power in my pockets. Trust me. I can make your lives a living hell."

I chuckle and shake my head. I give him a deadpan look. "Trust me when I say I don't give one fuck about you or the people you know." I breathe in through my nose. Spotting a cigar humidor sitting on the coffee table nearby, I walk over, lift the lid, and snag a few, shoving them into my pocket. "You see, Gates. I don't like you. Never have. And the fact that you're in town, sniffin' around Jo after fifteen years of no contact, makes me suspicious."

"Business with my daughter is none of your concern."

"Oh, but it is." I walk back and face him. "Jo is my family, which makes it my business." I pause a beat then continue. "I know why you're here and why you need that trust money so badly." His smug expression morphs, and his face tightens. "You're drowning in debt and looking at time behind bars for tax evasion if you don't pull something out of your ass."

"You know nothing." Gates juts out his chin.

"On top of that, your wife has been liquidating assets behind your back and filtering money into bank accounts you can't touch." I smirk when his smugness falters. "That's right. I'm guessing she found out what you were up to and decided to look out for herself." Gates doesn't say a word. "Want to guess whose name is on these secret bank accounts?" I ask and wait for him to say something. Gates looks at me, and I honestly think he has no clue. "Jonathan Stiles." I eye him as he puts two and two together. "I'm willing to bet your wife is fucking your number two guy, Gates. She's been screwing you and fuckin' the same son of a bitch I saw kissing Jo that night—the same motherfucker you claimed was going to be your future son in law." I chuckle again. "Funny how karma works."

"Fuck you!" Gates snarls, trying to rip himself from Wick's hold.

Nova, who is standing close by, exposes his gun for Jo's father to see. "Lower your fuckin' tone when talkin' to my brother."

"Are you fucking kidding me right now?" Gates looks from Nova to me, and I shrug. Now, I know we aren't going to kill the bastard. He's no threat to us. But I have no problem with Nova fucking with his head, either. He'll experience far worse panic and fear when he does time in prison.

"I don't want you here. Jo doesn't want you here. So, after our little conversation, you're going to pack your shit and leave my city."

"You think you can strong-arm me? I'm Richard Gates, you piece of shit." He puffs out his chest. "I don't see what she ever saw in you. Josephine is nothing more than a whore. Just. Like. Her. Mother."

I lose all composure, backhand him across the face, then just as fast pull my weapon. Gripping his face, I force the barrel of my gun in his mouth. His eyes widen like saucers. Fear is written all over his face. "I could put a bullet through the back of your head and still sleep easy tonight, with Jo at my side." Gates breathes heavily through his nose, his teeth chattering against the metal in his mouth. "You have no idea what I'm capable of. You see; my brother here—" I look at Wick then back at Gates "—is damn good at finding dirt on people. I could hand over enough evidence on you to put you away for a long time, Gates. Although, I suspect it will catch up to you soon enough without my help. After today I better not see your face again. You try to contact Jo or, God help you, my daughter, I'll kill you."

I shove the barrel a little further into his throat, causing him to gag. "You get the fuckin' picture?" Gates blinks, then finally agrees with a nod. "Good. Now get the fuck out of New Orleans." I rip my gun from his mouth, wipe it on his designer trousers then tuck it back in the holster at my side. Gates coughs a few times. I signal to my brothers it's time to leave by jerking my head toward the door. Before I walk out into the hall, I look back. "By the way, I made damn sure you could never get your hands on Jo's money." And I walk away.

18

JO

On the drive back to the house, my anger builds. So does my aggravation toward Sawyer. I know he's only trying to protect me, but I wanted to handle the situation with my father. There is still so much I want to say to him.

Tamping down the gamut of emotions swirling in my gut, I take a deep breath before climbing out of the car once I pull into the driveway. I don't even make it two steps inside the house before Sawyer throws herself at me like she's been waiting for me to walk through the door.

"Hey, Ladybug." I give my girl a genuine smile. Seeing her face, no matter how bad the day has been, always makes me happy.

"What's wrong?" she asks.

"What do you mean? Nothing is wrong." I usher her back through the door then close it behind me. Sawyer follows me into the kitchen, where I set my purse and keys down on the table.

"Don't do that, mom."

I turn toward Sawyer. "Do what?"

She huffs. "Treat me like a little kid. One minute everything is fine. Dad and I were getting ready to grill, and the next minute he was flying out the door. This was right after he talked to you. So, I know something is wrong."

"Ladybug," I say softly as I tuck a strand of her hair behind her ear.

"Mom, please. Tell me," Sawyer pleads.

Sighing, I nod for her to sit and take a seat beside her at the table. "I got a call from Aunt Maggie today. She told me my father was there looking for me. Then he showed up at the hospital. I was on the phone with your dad when it happened."

Sawyer gasps. Since she knows about the strained relationship, or lack of connection, with my father, the news is just as much a shock to her.

"What does he want?" she asks.

I shrug. "I don't know, sweetheart. I didn't get a chance to find out."

"Does Aunt Maggie know?"

"No. Aunt June chased him off with a shotgun." I bite my lip to keep from laughing, and I see Sawyer doing the same.

Then she turns serious again. "What's Dad doing?"

"I don't know that either. I trust him to take care of it, to take care of us."

Sawyer nods.

Over her shoulder, I see Genevieve round the corner of the hall into the kitchen with Everest at her side helping her. I jump from my chair and make my way to them. "Let me help you." I take hold of her other hand so she can lean into both me and Everest for better balance.

"Thank you." She smiles up at Everest once she's settled in a chair at the table and Everest takes off toward the living room. "I take it my son hasn't made it home yet?"

I shake my head. "I'm guessing you heard?"

"Yeah." Genevieve pushes her hand across the table, placing it on top of mine. "Are you okay?"

"Not really," I tell her honestly.

"Do you want to talk about it?"

I shake my head again. "Not really."

Genevieve nods and waits for a beat to ask, "Do you want some pot?"

Sawyer cups her hand over her mouth and giggles.

"Thanks, Genevieve," I chuckle. "But I'll have to pass."

Genevieve shrugs. "Let me know if you change your mind."

"I will," I say with a grin.

A COUPLE OF HOURS LATER, I'M SITTING ON THE FRONT PORCH WITH a glass of wine when Sawyer's bike rumbles to a stop in front of the house. Sawyer wanted to wait up with me because she was concerned, but I made her go to bed an hour ago since it's a school night. Genevieve went down shortly after.

Standing, I set my glass down on the table beside me, and I'm in front of Sawyer before he's entirely off his motorcycle. He doesn't waste any time wrapping his arms around me. As soon as I lay my head against his chest and breathe in his familiar scent, I can feel the tension I'm holding onto leave my body.

"Baby," Sawyer rasps, kissing the top of my head.

I close my eyes. "I'm not going to like what you have to tell me, am I?"

"Come on, let's go sit." Sawyer takes my hand and leads me back to the porch. Sitting in my vacant chair, he pulls me down to his lap. Cupping my face, Sawyer brushes his lips lightly against mine. "I love you."

Closing my eyes, I rest my forehead against his. "I love you too."

OVER THE NEXT SEVERAL MINUTES, SAWYER TELLS ME EVERYTHING.

"So, you're saying my father came here with the intent to trick me into signing some paper that would allow him to take the trust that lawfully belongs to me?" Suddenly, the anger I had before is nothing compared to what I'm feeling now.

"Yes," Sawyer confirms I indeed heard him right.

Jumping from his lap, I begin to pace back and forth. "Let me get this straight. That son of a bitch has run his company into the ground, gotten himself in trouble with the government?"

"Babe," Sawyer goes to say, but I continue to talk over him.

"For tax evasion!" I nearly shout.

"Jo, baby, calm down." Sawyer stands.

"I will not calm down."

"Babe." I feel Sawyer's fingers dig into my hips when he pulls me against his chest. "I handled it."

I look up at him. "You handled it?"

"Yeah. I handled it. Your dad isn't gettin' shit. I had Wick secure the trust, and I sent your dad packin'. By the time he gets back to Tennessee, the authorities will have everything they need and will be waitin' on him."

Stunned, I stare at Sawyer and process what he just said. "What?" I breathe.

"It's over." Sawyer's grip on me tightens. "He's no longer a concern."

Twisting out of his hold, I walk over to the edge of the porch and stare out into the night sky as I collect my thoughts. Sawyer basically just told me my father is probably going to prison, yet I feel no remorse. I mean, this is my father we're talking about, but I can't bring myself to care.

"Baby." Sawyer comes up behind me, and I can feel his heat on my back.

"I want to see him."

"No," he bites out.

I swing around and come face to face with Sawyer's hardened gaze.

"Sawyer," I try again. "I need this. I need closure."

Sawyer's body grows rigid, and for a second, I think he's going to say no.

"After we do this, that man doesn't get another second of your time. Letting the past dictate our future ends tonight."

"It ends tonight," I agree.

Pulling his phone from his pocket, Sawyer fires off a text followed by Everest stepping out of the house onto the porch. "Jo has somethin' she needs to take care of."

Everest jerks his chin. "I'll hold the fort down. Be safe, brother."

"Always." Sawyer grabs my hands and leads me toward his bike. "Let's go." He straddles his motorcycle, and I climb on behind him.

When we hit the highway, two other bikes roar in the distance. I look back over my shoulder to find Riggs and Wick. It's right then that I fully understand what the meaning of the word family truly is. Closing my eyes, I press my cheek against Sawyer's back and smile when I feel his hand squeeze my calf. All the nervousness I had swirling in the pit of my stomach when we left the house has vanished. It's because this man and his brothers have my back. I am not alone in this fight to reclaim what my father took from my daughter and me.

My eyes open when Sawyer lets off the throttle, and the bike slows as he turns into a parking lot. And that's when I see him walking out of the hotel. Immediately his eyes find mine. I don't make a move to get off the bike. Instead, I watch as my father's gaze flicks from me to Sawyer and to the two men with us. If I'm not mistaken, I'd swear I saw a flash of fear cross his face. But mostly, what I see is a man who has lost everything and knows it. I know that look all too well. I've had to see that same look staring back at me in the mirror every day for fifteen years. The day I lost Sawyer was the day I lost everything. I lost my soulmate, my daughter's father, my future. So, that look right there, the one currently etched on my father's face, is my closure. Karma took her sweet time on this one, but boy, did she make it worth the wait. And with that revelation, I smile. I smile and free my soul of the life I longed for, so long ago, so that I can make room for the blessings my future is sure to hold.

Done with giving that man any more of my time, I turn my attention to Sawyer, who has been gauging my reaction this whole time. "Let's go home."

Curling his hand around the back of my neck, Sawyer kisses the hell out of me. "You got it, baby."

I WAKE IN THE MIDDLE OF THE NIGHT TO THE SENSATION OF SAWYER'S beard rubbing against the skin on the inside of my thigh and open my eyes the exact moment his mouth finds my clit, making me gasp. My pussy is ultra-sensitive from the last two times he's been inside me tonight. After round two, Sawyer informed me it would be pointless to get dressed since he planned on fucking me again before the sun comes up. And he's making good on his promise. Not that I'm complaining.

"Sawyer," I pant, spreading my legs wider to give him better access.

The second Sawyer and I got home after seeing my father, he was on me. Something monumental transpired between us in that parking lot, something powerful. Sawyer and I reclaimed a piece of us that had been stripped away, and it was like he was trying to prove to himself and me that what we have now is real. We all have our own ways of how we deal. For example, some people need to talk, some people need silence and to be alone. Sawyer, I have learned, needs touch and closeness. It's not about sex and getting off. It's about connecting with me in a way only he can. It's about claiming. Over the past couple of weeks, I have caught Sawyer looking at me in a way that says if he doesn't keep me close, or if he's not touching me in some way, I'm going to disappear. And I get it. Because I have this fear I will wake up one day, and all of this will have been a dream.

"I'm coming." A gasp escapes past my lips when Sawyer inserts a finger, curling it upward against my g-spot. My legs begin to tremble as my orgasm starts to build.

"Not without me. I want your pussy squeezing my cock when you come." Sawyer slides his body up mine, making my skin prickle when his chest hair scrapes against my sensitive nipples. A satisfied sigh escapes my mouth when he pushes forward, sliding his thick cock inside me. As soon as the words are out of my mouth, he pulls away.

"Goddamn," Sawyer hisses, grinding his pelvis against my clit. "I gave you my dick twice already, and your pussy is still greedy."

"Mmm," I moan in response. And he's not wrong. I don't think I could ever get tired of having Sawyer inside of me.

"Faster," I urge, digging my heels into the back of his thighs.

"No." Sawyer keeps a slow, steady rhythm.

"Sawyer," I try again, thrusting my hips upward.

"Alright, baby," Sawyer says just before he pulls out of me and flips over on his back, taking me with him. "Now ride me," he demands, smacking my ass.

"Finally," I breathe. Not wasting any time, I take his heavy cock in my hand and line the head up, and as the tip of Sawyer's cock kisses the entrance of my pussy, I can't help but give him a taste of his own medicine. Biting my lip, I look down at the tortured look on his face and know he's barely hanging on by a thread.

A deep growl erupts from within his chest. "I said ride me." Sawyer's palm comes down on my ass cheek once again.

"Yes, sir." I lower myself onto his cock and hiss when he spanks my ass again three more times in succession. And if I didn't think it was possible to be any more turned on, Sawyer has proven me wrong.

"My baby likes to play," he says, grabbing my hips. "I think I'm going to have fun discovering just how much."

My pussy pulses around his cock at the thought of all the dirty things Sawyer has planned for me.

"Jesus fuckin' Christ," he growls. "You like that, don't you, baby?"

"Yes," I pant, digging my nails into his chest as I grind down on him.

"You're going to let me do whatever I want, aren't you?"

"Anything," I breathe.

"What about this?" Sawyer's hand slid down between the cheeks of my ass. "You going to let me have this too?"

Looking into his eyes, I tell him, "I'll give you anything."

"I fuckin' love you." He grips the hair on the back of my head. "Now come," he demands before stealing my breath with his mouth.

19

FENDER

Almost an entire month has come and gone since we sent Jo's father packing, and she hasn't heard from him since. There haven't been any immediate threats from the Reaper's Nomads recently, either. At least twice a week, the club hits the streets, looking for the fuckers. Lucky for them, they've stayed clear of New Orleans. The last known whereabouts of the unwanted biker club were reported two weeks ago by one of our contacts up in the delta area of Mississippi. He informed us they were spotted at a shithole hotel on the outskirts of a small town, and that the next day, they were gone. Even though they appear to be gone for good, we never fully let our guards down. For now, the club is still alert and making conscious efforts to maintain safety for our families and keep the riff-raff out of the city.

I stretch my arm, placing it behind my head. My slight movement causes Jo to snuggle closer at my side, cradling her head in the space between my shoulder and neck. How does a man like me get this lucky twice in his life? I shouldn't say twice. That would imply that I loved her twice, but the truth is, I never stopped loving Jo after falling for her years ago. She was—is my person. The one I'm meant to spend the rest of my life with. Reconnecting on a physical level is easy for us. It's the emotional shit we are still working on daily. We both recognize the years of hurt and heartache can't be washed away in a short amount of time. But, the love and deep, soulful connection we have for one another are stronger now than they ever were. We are worth fighting for.

Feeling Jo's lips pressed against my skin sends a signal straight to my dick. "Good morning," she whispers in a sleep-filled voice, and she kisses my lower neck area again. I wrap my arms around my woman and pull her on top of me.

"Mornin'." My hard-on rubs against her bare pussy.

"Well, hello." Jo gives a lazy smile. "Did I do that?" She plays coy as she wiggles against me. I respond by dragging her body up mine. Cupping one of her tits in the palm of my hand, I suck her nipple into my mouth. "Mmm," she moans, then gasps after I release it then move on to the other, giving it equal attention.

"You're fuckin' perfect." I palm both tits, pressing them together, then burying my face in her cleavage.

Jo laughs. "Did you just motorboat me?"

"Yes, ma'am." I look up at her and grin. "Now wrap that wet pussy around my cock, Jo."

Doing as she's told, my woman sits, then slides her ass back. She rubs her pussy down then up the shaft of my dick. "You're so fuckin' wet," I grind out. My eyes fixate on where our bodies are creating fiction. Jo pauses. Keeping her eyes trained on mine, she raises up on her knees, grips my cock, places it at her center, then slowly sinks down. "Fuck," I hiss as she takes all of me inside of her. I grip her hips and urge her to start moving. "That's it, baby." I let her take the lead.

"God, Sawyer, you feel so good." Jo throws her head back and her long silky hair brushes the tops of my legs. With the sudden urge to have her locks wrapped around my fist as I pound into her from behind, I pull her off my dick.

"Sawyer, what..."

"I want you on all fours. Now," I order.

Jo's breath catches in her throat and shivers at my command. Her amber eyes never leave mine as she steadies herself on her hands and knees.

"Arch your back and show me your pussy." I maneuver in behind her and fucking salivate at the sight of Jo's dripping wet pussy, bared and ready for my cock. Reaching up her back, I grab hold of her hair and wrap it around my fist. When I have a tight hold, I use my knee to nudge her legs further apart. Without warning her, I bring my palm upward, slapping her pussy.

Jo gasps, "Oh God."

I slap her pussy three more times, pleased as fuck when I feel how wet she's getting. "Fuckin' drenched," I growl, running my index finger through her folds.

"Sawyer, please," she begs, pushing her ass back.

"You want my cock, baby?" I take my dick and rub the head along her slit, teasing her.

"Sawyer!" Jo huffs.

I chuckle. "What is it, baby?"

"Stop teasing and fuck me."

"Like this?" I pull on Jo's hair, making her look back at me, and thrust forward, burying my cock inside her tight heat.

"Yes," she hisses.

"Fuck, your pussy fits me like a glove." Sweat drips down my back as I pound into her.

"I'm going to come."

"Damn, baby. I can feel it."

"Sawyer," she breathes. I feel her pussy begin milking my cock, and release the hold I have on her hair. I cup her tits in the palms of my hands and pull her back, bringing her flush against my chest.

"Come," I demand just before swallowing her cries with my mouth as we find our release together.

AFTER SHOWERING, JO AND I HEAD DOWNSTAIRS TO MY MOM'S ROOM. I knock, then enter her bedroom with Jo. As usual, Walter, her faithful hound dog is laying on the floor near the bed, basking in a ray of sunlight. "Mom." I find myself moving slower to catch the rise and fall of her chest. Relief washes over me upon realizing she's breathing. Jo walks around to the other side of the hospital bed we had put in a couple of weeks ago, because sleeping in an inclined position is more manageable for her breathing. "Mom?" I reach out and stroke her hair. Her eyes slowly open, and she licks her dry lips.

"You thirsty?" Jo asks, and Mom nods. She takes a sip of water through the straw.

"Thank you," Mom says, her voice weak. Jo then sets the cup down on the bedside table. Like I see her do every day since she and Sawyer have been living with me, she begins going through my mom's skincare routine by first using a cleansing wipe on her face, followed up with serums and creams.

"There." Jo smiles at her. "Beautiful as ever."

"You're a blessing, Jo. I hope you know that." Mom reaches out and takes hold of Jo's hand. "You and Sawyer have brought so much joy to my life in the past couple of months."

"You've been a joy in our lives, too, Genevieve."

Mom coughs then struggles to catch her breath. Both Jo and I hover, waiting for it to pass. "I'm okay," she assures us. Jo and I share a look of concern. We both know it is not alright. Mom's health has been on a steady decline, but she refuses to talk about it. Mom is determined to focus on each day she's given.

"Good morning, Grandma." Sawyer shuffles in with slept-in hair, yawning then climbs into bed beside Mom and pulls the blanket over her legs. "How are you feeling this morning? she asks.

"Grateful." Mom strokes Sawyer's hair. "How was your date last night?"

Sawyer cuts her eyes at me. "It was good. Jude and the team won their game."

"That's nice." Mom smiles when she looks at me and sees my tight expression. Jude is an okay guy for now, but I still don't like Sawyer dating.

"We went with a group of friends afterward. I went to Mad's house. Her mom cooked a bunch of food, so we ate and sat around a fire and just hung out for a while before Jude had to bring me home."

"Sounds like you had a good time," Mom says. "Promise me you'll make many more happy memories, sweetie." Mom shifts to kiss Sawyer on the top of her head, and her granddaughter looks up at her. The connection they share is deep. Has been since the day they met. A tear rolls down Sawyer's cheek, and I look at Jo as my mom says, "Don't cry, honey. It will be alright."

A FEW HOURS AFTER BREAKFAST, I WALK INSIDE TO CHECK ON MOM, leaving Jo and Sawyer fishing down by the lake. "Hey, Mom."

"Hey, sweetie."

"You need anything?"

Mom slowly moves the blankets off her legs, tossing them to the side of the bed. She tries getting out of bed on her own but fails to find the strength. She sighs. "I would love to get out of this bed."

Leaning down, I slide my arms beneath her knees and around

her torso and lift her into my arms. "Where would you like to go?" I ask.

"Take me outside."

"It's a bit cool today. Maybe I can set you up in the living room." I suggest, but Mom shakes her head.

"No. I want to breathe some fresh air into my lungs and feel the sun on my face." I nod and carefully grab the quilt off the foot of her bed. Mom drapes her thin arms around my neck and smiles. "Thank you."

Once outside, I set her down in an Adirondack chair facing the lake, with the sun on her face. Kneeling, I place the blanket on her lap. "You want anything? Some tea?"

Mom palms my cheek. I close my eyes briefly and lean into the touch. Her hand is warm. "You have made me so happy." I swallow hard and open my eyes. "I'm proud of you, son. You've done well for yourself and done well with the life you've been given. I'll also add that you're becoming a damn fine daddy to my granddaughter."

"I owe it all to you, Mom."

"Raising you was the most difficult yet fulfilling achievement of my life. I may have taught you how to spread your wings, but you are the one who was brave enough to fly." Mom caresses my face, and tears fill her eyes.

A considerable knot forms in the pit of my stomach, and my eyes sting from holding back my emotions. Why does it feel like she's saying goodbye?

"Daddy!" Sawyer shouts, and I look back over my shoulder to where she and Jo are standing on the dock. I watch her struggling to reel a catch in.

"She's got a big one." Mom laughs. "Go."

"I'll send Jo to sit with you." I stand.

"No. I'm fine. Just let me sit here and watch my family for a bit and feel the sun on my face," she says, her voice barely a whisper because she's so weak.

I smile. "Okay," I say, and turn toward the deck steps, but stop. I face my mom. "I love you." And somehow, the words feel different. They have a heaviness to them, like an anchor sitting at the bottom of the ocean floor.

"I love you too, son."

Leaving Mom to rest on the deck, I jog across the lawn and down the dock toward Sawyer and Jo, who is trying but failing at helping our daughter. "How can one fish be so strong?" The pole bends, putting too much strain on the line.

"Give him some slack. Let him run, then pull him back," I guide her. "You fight against the fish too much, you risk breaking the line with his resistance. You have to tire him out first."

"But won't he get away?" Sawyer asks as the fish take the line out.

"With luck, he won't. Now reel him in a little." I say, and my daughter does as instructed. "Repeat the process a few times if you have to, but let him run less and reel him in a bit more each time." I face Jo. "Can you grab the net hanging over there by the boat?" Jo walks over and snags the fishnet. "You remember how this goes." I kiss her while remembering the many times we went fishing when we were younger. "I taught your momma how to fish too," I say to Sawyer as she reels the line in a bit more. "That's it, baby girl. You've got him." Jo lowers herself to the dock, lying on her stomach.

"Get it, Mom!" Sawyer shouts, and Jo scoops the net into the water.

"He's too heavy. I need help before I fall," Jo grunts.

Getting on my knees, I reach down, wrap my hand around the handle of the net and hoist the fish out of the water.

"Holy shit, look how big he is," Sawyer says with excitement, and I chuckle.

"Sawyer. Language," Jo says with her stern mom voice.

"Sorry." Our daughter lays the fishing pole on the dock while I pull the hook from the fish's mouth. "What kind is it?"

"A largemouth bass. He looks to be around fifteen inches long," I get to my feet. Keeping the fish in the net, I hold it up. "I'd say he's at least a ten-pounder. Nice first catch."

"Thanks." Sawyer whips her phone out. "What did you catch your first time fishing, Mom?" Sawyer takes a picture of her mom and me with the fish, and I do my best not to laugh at the memory of Jo's first catch.

"A log," Jo says, and I burst with laughter. She swats at my arm playfully. "It was a big log." She pouts a little.

I pull Jo into my side. "You did reel it in all by yourself." I bite my lip to try and keep a straight face but fail. I kiss her forehead, her lips. "I was impressed."

Jo laughs. "It's a good memory."

"Yes, it is." I gaze at the speckles of gold around her pupils, then lean in for another taste of her mouth.

"Hey. I'm still here," Sawyer interrupts. "I want a picture with my fish." She holds out her phone for one of us to take. I take the phone, place it in my pocket, remove the net from around the fish and show my daughter how to hold him properly. Sawyer has the bass at her side, using both hands, and smiles. I hold her phone up and snap the first picture. Sawyer smiles as she poses for another photo. The wind blows, feeling like a hug as it swirls around me. On the phone, the screen sets my gaze upon my mom and I zoom in on her with the camera.

"Daddy?" I can see Sawyer lowering the fish to the dock. "Are you okay?"

"Sawyer." Even Jo's touch as her palm pressed gently against my back doesn't tear my eyes away. I just stand there knowing.

Jo looks at the camera, seeing I'm zoomed in on Mom. "Sawyer." Her whisper hints at knowing, too.

No matter how hard I try, I can't bring myself to say it. So, instead, I say, "She sleeps with the angels."

IT'S BEEN TWO DAYS SINCE MOM LEFT THE PHYSICAL WORLD. NOW, here we are, my entire family, plus Mom's best friend Amelia, all celebrating Mom's life at Pop's. Jo and the other women really did a great job putting it all together.

Needing some time to myself, I walk out to the water, where Pop tied his fishing boat to the dock, and step into it. I sit, pull one of Mom's joints from my pocket, and light it up. I inhale the hit deep into my lungs and let it burn before exhaling. After a few more hits, I feel relaxed enough to snub it out and save the rest for later. I look across the yard at my family. The kids are all running around playing while my brothers and their women sit around and talk shit about any topic besides death. My gaze shifts to my woman, who sits on the front porch beside Pop, in the same rocking chair my mom sat in weeks ago.

Death. It's hard and painful.

But only for those left behind.

It's a brutal reminder that we are alive and the one we lost is not.

I've been through a lot of shit in my life. Hardships are for the living. You can't avoid them. Sometimes we can't even control the outcome. But we wield power over how we choose to deal and react. I feel incredible sadness in the fact my mom is gone. At the same time, I have this overwhelming sense of relief knowing she's no longer in constant pain.

I pull my attention from my family and take in the nature surrounding me. The water is calm and the breeze is cool against my skin. A few yards away, perched on a log, is a blue heron, along with a few turtles basking in what's left of the day's sun before it gets swallowed by the bayou.

I hear footsteps approaching and turn my head. "Hey, honey." Amelia, Mom's best friend, is strolling toward me. "May I join you for a moment?" I reach up and give her my hand, helping her into the boat. She sits beside me. "How are you holding up?"

I pull in a lung full of air, feeling it's not enough. "I very much want to drown my grief in a bottle of whiskey." I allow myself to be candid.

Amelia nods. "That's fair."

"Not really."

She looks around. "Your mom would be filled with so much joy. You did well today."

I force a smile. "It all came together thanks to Jo and the club."

"I won't lie and tell you it gets easier because it doesn't. The truth is you adapt. The grief you feel becomes a part of life. Some days missing them may not feel as strong, but their absence is still felt." Amelia sighs. "I'm going to miss her so much." She reaches into her back pocket and hands me a folded-up envelope. "It's from your mom." I look at my name, scribed in her handwriting on the back. "She realized that she wasn't going to beat cancer this time well before the doctors confirmed it. So, your mom began planning for the next chapter of life. Her death and its aftermath. She wrote this letter a few weeks ago, just before she started declining, and mailed it to me with strict instructions not to give it to you until after her passing." I hesitate to open the letter.

"Hey." Jo walks up.

"Hey, Jo." Amelia looks up and smiles at her, then back at me, saying, "I'll take my leave." I stand and help her out of the boat. Amelia embraces Jo for a moment then walks away.

A chilling wind blows, and Jo hugs herself. "I just wanted to check on you. I'll leave you..."

"Stay." I hold out my hand. Jo takes it, and I help her into the boat, having her sit beside me.

"Nice view." She gazes out at the water. Her eyes fall on the envelope in my hand. "What's that?"

"A letter Mom wrote weeks ago." I open the envelope, pull out the paper, and unfold the letter. With Jo at my side, I read it.

Son,

If you're reading this, I'm sleeping with the angels.

Even when we expect it, and we're facing our own mortality, death is a surprise. Mainly because we don't always know the exact moment it will happen. I admit I was afraid to die. I was never going to be ready. It would never be the right time, but I made peace with it, nonetheless. The hardest part is leaving the ones I love behind and knowing a great sadness will follow after I am gone. The pain you will be left with makes leaving hard to bear.

Just know, you are the greatest gift life gave to me. Sleepless nights, dirty diapers, scraped knees, and runny noses... I would do it all again. I love you past the moon and stars, Son. Don't forget that. I'm so proud of the man you've become.

Tell Jo she is loved.

Tell my granddaughter to never stop singing and to reach for the stars.

From here on, promise me one thing. Don't forget how to live and to love. You and Jo have something special. And I was there to witness you realizing how much you love her still.

Have fun.

Share lots of laughs.

Don't sweat the small stuff.

Make memories to last more than one lifetime.

Before we know it, time slips through our fingers. Never miss a single moment, because you can never get it back.

And Sawyer... have babies. Lots of babies. Fill your house with so much love it bursts at the seams.

If I could ease the pain of my absence, I would. I'd wrap you in a hug only my arms could deliver.

Hold on tight, Sawyer. Remember, just because you can't feel my embrace doesn't mean I ever let you go.

LOVE, MOM.

20

JO

The sun begins to set beyond the bayou, bringing an end to a chapter in our lives that will forever leave an imprint on our souls. The celebration of life that was held for Sawyer's mom was beautiful. However, watching my daughter and the man I love struggle with their grief makes me feel helpless. Because there is nothing I can say or do that will alleviate that pain. Witnessing my daughter's heartbreak for her grandmother fills my heart with sorrow. My girl was robbed of so much time. I can't help but think of all the years and memories missed that she'll never have with her grandmother. Oh, but she and Genevieve spent these past several weeks making up for time lost. It was a beautiful thing watching how naturally the two connected. One thing Genevieve did was make sure her granddaughter knew how much she was adored and loved. They may not have had time on their side, but what memories they did make will be cherished forever.

"How are you holding up, Ladybug?" I wrap my arms tighter around Sawyer, who has her head resting against my chest as she stares out at the water.

She sniffles. "I'm okay."

It kills me how small her voice sounds. "Come on." I kiss the top of her head. "Let's go check on your dad." Keeping my arm around her shoulders, Sawyer and I make our way down the dock. Just as we start making our way across the yard, a familiar truck drives down the driveway and parks behind Pop's truck.

"Aunt Maggie, Aunt June!" Sawyer cries, breaking free from me. She makes a mad dash across in their direction, and I watch as they both brace for Sawyer's impact as she throws herself into their arms.

"Hey, sweetheart." Aunt Maggie gives me a warm smile and pulls me into her arms as soon as I'm within arm's reach.

"You didn't have to come," I tell her.

Aunt Maggie pulls back and tucks a strand of hair behind my ear. "Yes, we did," she says. "You're my girl, Jo. I'll always be here for you."

"And I love you for it." I give my aunt a small smile.

"Baby," Sawyer calls out.

I look over my shoulder to see a curious look on his face as he strides toward us.

"Dad!" Sawyer runs up to her father and throws her arms around his neck. After a quick embrace, she grabs his hand. "Come meet my aunts."

I turn back to Aunt Maggie and Aunt June to see them both holding back their emotions as they watch the way Sawyer acts with her dad and the clear adoration they have for each other.

"Aunt June, Aunt Maggie, this is my dad, Sawyer."

"Ma'am." Sawyer offers his hand to Aunt Maggie first.

Aunt Maggie shakes her head. "I won't have any of that damn nonsense. We're family. You can call me Maggie, and this is my wife, June."

"It's good to meet you, Maggie and June. Jo and Sawyer talk about you two all the time."

"We've heard an awful lot about you too." Aunt June smiles. "Our Ladybug goes on and on about you every time she calls."

"Does she now?" Sawyer pulls his daughter into his side and kisses the top of her head.

"Oh, yeah," Aunt June continues. "We heard all about the movie theater incident."

My daughter giggles, but Sawyer just smirks. Leave it to Aunt Maggie to find a way to lighten the mood.

"Why don't y'all come inside, and I'll introduce you to everybody," I suggest.

NIGHT HAS FALLEN, THE SKY IS CLEAR, AND THE STARS ARE SHINING brighter than I've ever seen since moving to New Orleans. Shortly after my aunts arrived, Sawyer and I took them around and introduced them to his family. Like I knew they would be, they were all welcoming, and not one person batted an eye when Aunt Maggie introduced Aunt June as her wife. And watching them fit in comfortably now as we all sit around the fire and share stories makes my heart full. I fully intend to take it as a sign that Genevieve is making her presence known and enjoying how beautiful the moment is.

The sound of Tequila laughing draws me from my wandering thoughts. "Are you serious?" She throws her head back and laughs while holding her pregnant belly. "Damnit, I'm going to pee myself again."

"It's true." Sawyer giggles. "Tell them, Mom. Dad totally ambushed my date."

"Fender, you didn't." Promise looks at him with a shocked expression. "Her first date?"

My body starts to shake with his when he lets out a chuckle. "How come you guys aren't givin' Kiwi hell like you are me. He was there too?"

"What!" Piper gasps and looks to her man, who is giving Sawyer a death glare for outing him.

"Snitch," Kiwi grumbles.

"Hey, man. If I'm going down, I'm takin' your ass with me."

"You two should be ashamed of yourselves," Piper admonishes.

Luna pokes at Riggs, who seems to be enjoying the show, then she begins to sign, and Nova translates. "I'll kick your butt if you ever pull a stunt like that with our daughter."

Riggs lets out a bark of laughter. "Sorry, baby. I'll just have to take whatever ass kickin' is comin' my way. You might as well start now, cause if I have my way, our baby girl won't be datin' until she's thirty," he declares.

"Neanderthals," Tequila huffs. "Every one of you." Then she looks at Sawyer. "Don't worry, girl. Stick with us, women. We know how to keep these loons in check."

After the conversation steers in a different direction, I cut my eyes over to Aunt Maggie to find her smiling at me. It's a smile that says she more than approves of the people I now call family.

"Mom," Sawyer calls out, and I divert my attention.

"What is it, Ladybug?"

"Did you remember to bring my guitar?"

"Yes. It's in the trunk of the car."

"I'm going to go get it. I told Aunt Maggie I'd play that song Dad has been teaching me." She jumps up from her chair and looks at her father. "Will you sing it with me, Dad?"

Sawyer, not being able to deny his daughter, smiles. "Anything you want, baby girl."

"Awesome!" She takes off toward where my car is parked.

A LITTLE WHILE LATER, I GO TO CLIMB OFF SAWYER'S LAP WHEN HE stops me.

"Where you goin'?" he asks.

"I'm going to get another beer. You want one?"

"Yeah, baby. I'll take another."

Leaning down, I give him a kiss. "Be right back."

Sawyer grips the back of my neck and stares into my eyes for a moment, then lets me go. "Hurry back."

When I step onto the porch leading into Pop's house, I run into Riggs and Luna. When Luna spots me, she waves and smiles. Then I watch as she signs something to Riggs. Riggs turns to me. "Luna wants to ask how you're doing and if there is anything you or Sawyer need?"

I make sure to face Luna and not Riggs when I reply so that she can read my lips, even though her husband translates. "Thanks for asking. I'm doing okay, and I think my aunts being here has gone a long way in helping Sawyer."

Riggs continues to sign. "Your aunts are great. I'm so happy they're here."

"Thanks, Luna. That means a lot."

Luna turns back to Riggs, and they exchange a few more words before she takes off back toward the fire pit where everyone is lounging. I don't miss how Riggs hangs around with me. I also pay attention to how his eyes don't leave his wife until she has made it all the way across the yard and seated next to Pop, who is holding their sleeping daughter. Something I have noticed about the Kings men is they treat their women like queens and hold them above all others. The bond this MC—this family—has is like no other. And as I stare at the family gathered around the fire, smiling, drinking, sharing stories of the past and present, and clinging to each other in this time of grief, it is not lost on me how incredibly blessed I am to be a part of it.

"You're fortunate," I say, feeling Riggs' eyes on me but not taking mine off my daughter, who is running around the giant oak tree off to the side of Pops' house, chasing fireflies with Sydney and Promise's little boy.

"I am," Riggs agrees. "There is nothing more important than family. And I'm not talkin' about the family you share blood with. I'm talkin' about the kind of family that's sittin' out there." Riggs jerks his chin in the direction of the laughter. Then he adds, "We're your family too, Jo. Just want ya to know that. There's not a person here who wouldn't do anything for you or your daughter."

I look at Riggs and try but fail to hold back how much his words mean to me. "Thank you, Riggs." My voice shakes. "I'll never be able to express how much that means to me. To know that the people Sawyer cares about the most welcomed my daughter and me the way you all did."

"Just speakin' the truth, darlin'. I've known Fender for a long time. Never seen him as happy as he's been since you and his daughter came back into his life. I'm fuckin' grateful to see my brother get what I know he deserves." On that note, Riggs takes his leave and makes his way to his wife and daughter.

A few minutes later, I'm stepping out of the house with two beers in hand when I run into Promise, who has her little boy on her hip.

"Hey."

"Hey, Jo. Just coming to get this little terror cleaned up."

I look at her son, who looks like he decided to sit in a mud puddle, and I laugh. "Need any help?" I ask.

"Actually, I do. Do you mind grabbing his bag from the back seat of my car? I have a change of clothes in there."

"Sure. I'll be right back." Setting the beers down on the table beside the front door, I jog down the porch steps and head in the direction of the parked cars. Reaching the back passenger door of Promise's sedan, I've just opened the door when there is a loud popping noise out of nowhere. It sounds like someone setting off fireworks. Just as I look over my shoulder, the car's back window explodes, sending shards of glass flying all around me. "Oh my God!" I yelp and drop to the ground when a sharp burning sensation rips through my thigh. From that moment on, everything seems to happen in slow motion. Several men come out of nowhere, emerging from the treeline with their guns raised. I watch in horror as the men start shooting anywhere and everywhere. Hearing the fear in my daughter's voice as she cries out for me has me ignoring the pain in my leg, and I'm on my feet in a flash.

"Sawyer!" I scream when I spot her lying on the ground behind a large tree. Her father spots her as well. I ignore the mayhem surrounding me as I start to run toward them. I make it two feet before I'm grabbed from behind and slammed to the ground with so much force that it knocks all the air from my lungs.

"Grab the bitch and let's go!" someone shouts.

"Prez said he wanted one of the kids," another man says, and I look up to see a large, bearded man, with a pale complexion and a greasy mop of brown hair hanging in his face, standing over me.

Kids? What's going on? Oh, God. Do these men want to kidnap one of our children?

"Too fuckin' bad. Now let's go," the same man orders.

And while the two of them are arguing, I try to make a run for it, but before I can even lift myself off the ground, the large man turns his dark, empty eyes to me.

"Where do you think you're going, cunt?" he sneers just before lifting his leg and bringing his booted foot down on my face, making everything go black.

21

FENDER

Gunfire explodes around us.

"Down, down, down!" Riggs barks. Women hit the ground, shielding the children close by with their bodies as our men aim in the direction the bullets are coming from. I look around for Jo, hoping like hell she's still inside the house. My head jerks to where Sawyer was hanging out with Sydney by the giant oak tree.

Several bullets whiz past my head as I dash across the yard toward my daughter.

Wick rushes in the same direction, going after his niece. My stomach tightens hearing Sawyer screaming for her mom and me. "Daddy! Mom!"

"Get down!" I shout, but my warning comes too late. I watch Sawyer take a bullet and fall to the ground. My heart stops. *No.* I run faster. The moment I reach her, I fall to my knees. Wick covers Sydney with his body.

"Where's Aunt Vayda?" A bullet ricochets off the side of the tree trunk. Wick's body muffles Sydney's voice as he keeps her shielded beneath him.

"No, no, no. Don't fuckin' do this." I curse the heavens. "Baby girl." I turn her over, instantly seeing blood soaking through the waistband of her jeans. Sawyer cries out in agony, her hands go to the source of her pain on her lower abdomen.

"Daddy. It hurts."

I stay behind the shelter of the tree as gunfire continues. "I know, baby. I know." I quickly scoop my daughter into my arms. As quickly as the gunfire began, it stops. It's only a second later that Riggs is shouting.

"Get the women and children inside!"

Wick scoops his niece into his arms. Sydney looks at Sawyer. "Sawyer?" She tears up. "What's wrong with Sawyer?"

Neither Wick nor I answer. I gather my daughter into my arms and race toward the house.

"Where's my mom?" Sawyer sobs, but I don't answer her. My feet hit the porch, stepping on shattered glass from the nearby window.

Pop is standing on the porch two feet from me, with his rifle aimed in the direction the attacking gunfire was coming from. His attention shifts to me long enough for his eyes to drop and notice the blood. "Bad?"

"Yeah," I say, then follow Wick into the house.

"Fender!" Piper runs up to me as I lay Sawyer on the living room sofa. "Oh my God!"

"I need a towel or something." I push Sawyer's hands away from the wound area, but she resists. "I'm sorry, sweetheart, but we need to apply pressure."

"Daddy, I'm scared."

"I know." I look around for Piper and Luna appears, holding Riggs' hand and her little girl on her hip. She kneels beside my daughter and strokes her hair. It's a simple gesture. A mother's touch, even if it isn't Jo's, helps. Other family members begin to rush into the house, including Amelia and Jo's aunts.

"Sawyer!" her Aunt June cries and comes to stand at the back of the sofa. "She's been shot," she says, shocked.

"I want my mom!" my daughter cries out.

Piper is quickly back at my side with a towel, and I press it firmly against my daughter's lower abdomen. I look at Piper. "Apply as much pressure as she can stand. I need to find Jo." Piper immediately jumps into action.

Riggs appears at my side, stopping me in my tracks. I feel his hand on my shoulder. "Jo is gone."

"What do you mean she's gone?" I hold my breath.

"Reaper's Nomads took her," Riggs says, and I feel the world crumbling beneath my feet. Riggs continues, "Everest just phoned. He gave chase as soon as the gunfire ceased. Once he got about a mile down the road, he saw them transferring Jo from one vehicle into another. They fired at him. Everest lost control of his bike and had to leave it in the ditch."

"Brother, Sawyer needs to get to the hospital. She has internal bleeding." I jerk my head at Wick's tense warning.

Ignoring everyone, I scoop Sawyer off the sofa and back into my arms.

"Wait, where are you going?" June's strained voice cries as she follows me out of the house.

"To the hospital." I bound down the porch steps toward my car.

"I'm going." June helps by opening the car door. She slides into the back seat, and I carefully lay Sawyer beside her. "Keep pressure on the wound." I place June's hand on the towel. Maggie jumps into the front passenger's seat as I'm climbing behind the wheel. I put the key in the ignition. "Did he say which way they're headin'?" The car's engine roars.

"East," Riggs informs me, then backs away just before I press the accelerator into the floorboard. I leave Pop's house in a cloud of dust in the rearview mirror as I take off down the road. Once on the highway, I open the engine and gun it.

. . .

AFTER BREAKING THE SPEED LIMIT AND RUNNING SEVERAL RED lights, I peel into the hospital parking lot, bringing the car to a stop outside the emergency room doors. Jumping out, I reach into the back seat, scoop my daughter into my arms again and carry her through the double doors. "We need help," Maggie shouts to get some attention, and the triage nurse rushes toward us.

"We need a gurney over here," she shouts. "What happened?" She notices the blood-soaked towel cradled against my daughter's pelvic area.

"Gunshot." I lay her on the bed, and the nurse and one other begin wheeling her away. "How old is she?"

"Fifteen."

"We need a doctor in trauma one!" the nurse orders while removing the towel and tossing it into a bin. She asks my daughter, "What's your name, sweetheart?"

"Sawyer," she moans.

"And you are?" The nurse cuts her eyes at me.

"Her father."

The other nurse begins cutting away at Sawyer's clothes. "I'm going to have to ask you to step out, Mr....?"

"Like hell. I am not leaving my daughter," I growl.

"Mr. Huntington?" I recognize the voice and spin around to find Dr. Ledger. His eyes drop to my blood-soaked shirt, then he looks around me. He jumps into action. "What do we have?"

"A gunshot wound to the lower left of the pelvic region. No exit wound." The nurse relays her assessment so far. "Her vital signs are good."

Dr. Ledger examines my daughter. "She has abdominal distention." Then he presses around Sawyer's lower abdomen, and my daughter groans. "Call up to the OR and tell them we are on our way."

By now, the nurses have my daughter hooked up to monitors, and an IV line started. Beside me, Jo's aunts hold each other. Dr. Ledger removes his gloves. "We need to find the source of the bleeding."

"I can't believe this is happening," Maggie whispers. "Can we see her for a second?" She looks at Dr. Ledger.

"Of course." Then he turns his attention back on me. "Where's Jo?" he asks, not knowing the weight of his questioning.

The words are hard to force past my lips. "She's on her way."

Another nurse arrives. "The OR is ready for you, Dr. Ledger."

"I'll have a nurse keep you updated. You can wait in the family room." Dr. Ledger moves to exit the room, but I stop him.

"Don't let her die."

"She'll be alright, Mr. Huntington." I step to the side, and he leaves.

The nurses unlock the gurney wheels, and I follow beside my daughter, holding her hand as she's rolled down the hall. Sawyer's eyes open and close. "Daddy, I feel funny."

"It's probably the medicine they gave you, baby girl." Before they load Sawyer onto the elevator, her aunts kiss her cheek and tell her *I love you*. Then, I lean down and kiss her forehead. "I'll be here when you get back."

"Daddy."

"Yeah, baby girl?"

"I want my mom."

Her words feel like the weight of the world being placed on my shoulders. "I'll bring her home," I vow.

After the elevator door closes, I help the aunts find the waiting room. "I need to step out for a moment."

Both aunts look at me. June says, "We'll hold the fort down here and call should anything change." I nod and walk out of the room.

As I step into the emergency room waiting area, I'm met by Riggs, Nova, and Kiwi. "How's Sawyer?"

"All vital signs are good, but she's bleeding internally. They took her up to the OR a few minutes ago." Needing some fresh air, I walk out of the hospital toward my car, and they follow me. "Where's Wick—the family?" I rummage through the glove compartment in search of a cigarette. I pull one from the pack I find and light it. The burning in my lungs as I hold in the smoke and nicotine does nothing to calm the storm brewing inside me.

"Wick went to pick up Everest, then do some scouting to find these sons of bitches. And the family is camped out at Pop's with Catcher helping him keep watch over everyone."

"We can't just sit on our asses." I run my fingers through my hair. I'm barely hanging on by a thread. Within forty-eight hours, I've lost my mom, my daughter is lying on an operating room table, and the love of my life is in the hands of Reaper's Nomads.

"I understand your frustration, brother. You'll get your chance at vengeance, and we'll get your woman back in the process," Riggs says.

Everything I'm feeling comes to a head and explodes. An inferno swirls in my gut. I let out a guttural roar, then put my fist through the glass. Half of the car window shatters, and the jagged edges cut against my skin.

I pull my hand back, my knuckles bloodied. I absorb the pain, using it to add fuel to the rage growing inside of me.

We turn our heads at the sound of Harleys approaching to see Wick, along with Everest, rolling into the parking lot. Everest is on a different ride than his own. They cut the engines. "We found them," Wick says.

"Where?" I toss my cigarette to the ground.

"Less than two hours from here in a shit hotel," Wick informs us.

"Sawyer!" I turn around as my name is shouted, and Maggie is jogging toward us. She stops. "They called with an update on our girl. They found the source of bleeding. The doctor says she is doing well and should be in recovery within the hour."

I let out a heavy sigh of relief, knowing my daughter will be alright. "Thanks, Maggie. Listen, I need to go."

Maggie throws her hand up. "Say no more. We'll be there by Sawyer's side when she comes out of surgery." She glances around at each man beside me then brings her attention back to me. "You go out there and bring our Jo back." She gives me a confident smile and turns back toward the hospital

I look at my brother. "Let's get my woman back." With no time to waste, Riggs, Nova, and Kiwi jump on the back of their bikes, and I jump into my car.

22

JO

"Prez is going to be fuckin' pissed. I told you he wanted one of the kids."

"Yeah, well, Prez wasn't there, asshole. You saw for yourself; there was no way we were snatchin' one of those little bastards. Hell, I almost got a bullet in my ass twice. And where the hell were you, Bash? Did you grow a pussy again and bail like you did last time?"

"Man, fuck you, Screw."

I have been lying in the backseat of some car for I don't know how long listening to two men argue back and forth. Neither one has noticed I'm awake, and I am doing everything within my power to keep my breathing level and stay still, so I don't draw any attention toward myself. I'm still confused, but so far, by what pieces I've put together, the men are members of another MC. I can't believe their intentions were to kidnap one of the children. And despite how terrified I am right now, I'm thankful it was me and not one of the kids.

A phone ringing interrupts the argument the men are having.

"Yeah," one guy answers. "Fuck!" he roars.

I flinch at what sounds like a fist hitting the dashboard.

"Fuck, Screw. What is it, man?" the other man asks.

"That was Tiny. He said they lost Dime and Chains. He says they went down and they didn't have time to get them out of there."

"Damnit, Prez is going to flip his shit."

"We need to get our story straight before we get back to the hotel."

"What the hell are we supposed to say?"

"I don't fuckin' know. Damn, Bash."

The two men are silent for a moment.

"Look. Those bastards probably have Chains and Dime. They're as good as dead. We just tell Prez they got trigger happy and went in too soon; they blew the whole operation. I'll just tell him we had no choice but to snatch one of their old ladies."

"Shit, Screw. That's fuckin' low."

"You got a better idea, asshole? It's either we go with that, or Prez puts a bullet in both our heads."

"You're fuckin' crazy, man."

"Just stick to the goddamn story, you pussy."

The car comes to a stop, and my heart rate begins to pick up. The men still haven't noticed me, and a thought comes to mind. I'm going to try and make a run for it.

A second later, both men exit the car, and instead of immediately coming for me, I hear them start talking to another guy. It's dark outside, but when I tip my head back slightly, I see the three men huddled together next to the front passenger side door. With them in deep conversation about something, I take this opportunity to try and get away.

While keeping my eyes on the men, I slowly lift my hand to the back door handle. Once it's in my grip, I pull. The door makes a clicking sound, and I pause. When the men still don't look, I quickly throw the door all the way open and bolt. Ignoring the searing pain in my leg, I concentrate on putting one foot in front of the other as I run. Nothing about my surroundings is familiar, but at this point, what direction I run is not essential so long as it's away from those men.

Across the street, about fifty yards in front of me, I spot a gas station. A man stands next to his truck with his back to me, pumping gas. As I open my mouth to scream for help, someone rams into me from behind, and the two of us slam into the pavement. I cry out when I'm flipped onto my back and backhanded across the left side of my face.

"Fuckin' cunt," the bald man straddling me spits.

"Let me go!" I bring my arms up to block my face from the next blow.

"Damnit, Bash. Get the bitch inside before somebody sees and calls the cops." I hear boots crunching on the gravel next to my head as one of the other bikers rushes over.

"Get your ass up." The man who hit me grips a handful of my hair and pulls me up off the ground.

"Fuck you." I try twisting out of his hold while bringing my foot up and kicking the hell out of his knee, making the asshole lose his grip on me and causing him to fall.

My second attempt to escape is also short-lived. One of the other men grabs the back of my neck in a vise-like grip just before landing a punishing blow to my stomach. It knocks all the wind from my lungs, making me sputter and cough. I desperately try to fill my lungs with air.

"Bash, get your pansy ass up and get this bitch inside," he orders.

"And you." The fingers around my neck tighten as the man, who I now recognize as the one who knocked me out at Pop's, leans in close. I can smell the beer and cigarettes on his hot breath. "You try runnin' again, and you'll be beggin' for death by the time I get done playin' with you."

"Yeah," I wheeze, still trying to recover from his assault. "I could say the same thing to you. Because that's exactly what you'll be doing when the Kings find you."

For a split second, I think I see a flash of fear cross the guy's face, but it's quickly replaced with a smirk. "We'll just have to see about that."

"Tie her up." The bald asshole pushes me forward, making me stumble when we walk into the hotel room. Bash then shoves me down onto a chair and proceeds to tie my hands behind my back, and then binds each of my ankles to the chair's legs.

As the minutes tick by, the three bikers grow more and more anxious. The bald man keeps peeking through the curtains, and the other two just stare off into space while chain-smoking. It doesn't take long before the rumble of several motorcycles can be heard making their way into the parking lot. For a split second, I get my hopes up, but they are quickly replaced with dread when the guy watching out the window announces, "Prez is here."

"About fuckin' time." The one they call Bash jumps to his feet. A second later, the door to the hotel opens. A man walks in. One look sends a cold chill down my spine. He doesn't acknowledge the other men when he strides in; instead, his predatory gaze lands directly on me.

"Who do you belong to?" he asks.

I take a moment to study the man in front of me. He's not very tall, standing at maybe five feet, eleven inches. He has a receding hairline, and what little, greasy hair he does have hangs limp around his shoulders. The man does have broad shoulders but a pudgy belly. My eyes flick down to the patch on the front of his leather vest. *President.*

I look at him before opening my mouth. "I don't belong to anyone."

The slap comes out of nowhere. I grit my teeth to keep from saying more to piss the man off. "Don't get fuckin' smart cunt," he sneers.

"Which one of those pussy Kings is your old man?"

Giving the man a look of disdain, I say, "Fuck you." I know my answer will only anger him further and cause more pain, but there is no way I will tell these men anything about my family.

What comes next happens so fast, I have no time to prepare. Bash pulls a filthy bandana from his back pocket, shoves it in my mouth, pulls a blade from his boot, then brings it down into my thigh, driving it straight through my flesh.

"Ahhh!" I scream behind the cloth in my mouth, and the man behind me presses his palm over my mouth to further muffle my cries.

Through the pain, my face breaks out into a cold sweat and I struggle to swallow down the bile that's rising in the back of my throat.

"Now, let's try this again." The President bends at the waist and pulls the bandana from my mouth. "Which one of those mother fuckers is your old man?"

Breathing deep through my nose, I fight through the urge to throw up. "Go. Fuck. Yourself." My words are muffled, but the bikers understand every syllable.

"Fuckin', bitch." He shoves the bandana back in my mouth, grips the knife still wedged in my thigh, pulls it out then pierces my other leg with it.

I wail and sob behind the hand clamped over my mouth as I thrash and struggle against the binds around my wrists in a desperate attempt to break free. I yank and pull so hard that I can feel trickles of blood seeping down my hands and fingers.

"You know what? It doesn't matter which one of those pussies you belong to because, in the end, they will read my message loud and clear when I return you to them in pieces." His words are said with so much hate that I fear he means every word. The menacing look in his eyes says he does.

"Still feelin' loyal, bitch?" The man grabs my hair and yanks my head back as he leans in close to my face. "Hmm? How does it feel knowin' you're going to die for those pieces of shits?"

I refuse to answer his question. Instead, I look him dead in the eyes and let my silence speak for itself, which only seems to anger him more.

"Answer me, bitch!" he bellows, spittle flying from his mouth. "Your precious Kings think they own this city."

I whimper when he withdraws the knife from my leg.

"They think they can kill my men and get away with it." He raises his arm in the air in a way that looks like he's about to backhand me but instead, he brings the blade down, slicing across my chest from one shoulder to the other.

He doesn't muffle my cries this time.

MY PANTS AND SHIRT ARE SOAKED WITH BLOOD. WITH EACH SECOND that ticks by, my body grows colder, and I suddenly have a hard time keeping my eyes open. If this keeps up, I will either pass out from pain or blood loss. I pray someone hears me and calls the police.

"Prez, we have company." The windows in the hotel room begin rattling from the approaching motorcycles.

"What do we do, Prez?"

"It's showtime," he answers. "Untie her."

Fingers tug roughly at the binds around my wrists, making me grit my teeth. Once free, a cold, tingling sensation shoots up my arms.

"Let's go." Bash wraps his meaty palm around my bicep, pulls me to my feet, and shoves me forward toward the door. His

President then maneuvers my body in front of him like a human shield.

The moment we step out the door, my knees buckle. I'm so weak, I can hardly hold myself upright. "Stand the fuck up." The arm around my waist tightens.

I first see Sawyer and breathe a sigh of relief, and a calmness washes over me. Finding all the strength I can muster, I stand. When Sawyer locks eyes on me, pure rage and agony cross his face.

"Sawyer," I whimper.

"You're fuckin' dead," Sawyer seethes, aiming his gun at the man behind me.

It's then I notice Riggs, Nova, Wick, Kiwi, and Everest too. Every man in the parking lot has his gun drawn and aimed at each other.

23

FENDER

Guns are drawn. Every man has another in his crosshairs, ready and willing to pull the trigger. We're in a standoff with Reaper's Nomads, and their president has my woman in his grasp.

My eyes travel over Jo's disheveled state. Her shirt hangs off one shoulder, exposing a knife slash that spans across her upper chest. My nostrils flare while breathing heavily through my nose. They put their dirty hands on my woman and hurt her. Blood coats her clothes—too much blood. My fingers flex against the cold metal of my gun, itching to put a bullet in the bastard's head. Jo sways, but her amber eyes stay locked on mine. I take a couple of steps forward, and the motherfucker presses the barrel end of his gun hard against Jo's cheek, causing her to whimper. "It appears we have something of great value to you." He smirks, then leans in and sniffs my woman's hair. "Something as pretty smellin' as she is." His tongue darts past his lips like a snake. Jo tries pulling away, but the bastard tightens his hold on her. "I bet her pussy tastes good too." The hand gripping her waist moves further down Jo's body.

"You're dead," I growl.

The son of a bitch laughs. "You are in no position to make threats."

Every muscle in my body twitches with a need for vengeance. I want to murder the men responsible for what has happened today, and every one standing before us. The president grabs Jo's hair, wrenching her head backward, but keeps her held out in front of him. "Only a fuckin' coward hides behind a woman," I seethe.

"Fuck you!" He yanks on Jo again, and she cries out.

"Sawyer," she whimpers, and her knees buckle.

"Stand the fuck up, cunt," the Reaper's Nomads president growls, having to hold Jo's body weight himself.

Riggs speaks, keeping his gun raised and ready to fire. "What do you want, you piece of shit?"

The son of a bitch huffs. "What do I want?" He laughs bitterly. "This bastard wants to know what it is we want." He looks around at his men, then back at Riggs. "We've buried some of our men because of you motherfuckers." His voice becomes louder. "And one of them—our vice president—was my *son!*" he rages. "It's only fittin' your club pays the price. An eye for an eye. And this bitch—" He shoves Jo again. "Will pay for your sins."

Tension ripples through me. I won't let Jo die. "I killed your bastard son, you son of a bitch," I confess, keeping my gun trained on him. His eyes widen, and his nostrils flare with anger. "You want someone to pay, then that someone is me."

"Goddamnit," Riggs mumbles, but doesn't interfere with my decision. He would do the same for his woman.

"You men hear this shit? This fucker is willin' to trade his life for the bitch," he laughs, and the others snicker along with him. Then he's silent for a beat. "Alright. You for the whore." I take a step forward. "Now, hold on, lover boy. This is how our little transaction is goin' down. You're goin' to drop that gun to the ground." I hesitate for a second, and the fucker jams the end of his weapon against Jo's ribcage. "Do it," he orders, and I let my gun slip from my grasp. "Now kick it away." I shove it across the asphalt with the toe of my boot. "After the exchange, the rest of you get on your fuckin' bikes, pack up your shit, and get the hell out of New Orleans." He eyes Riggs. "This is my city now." Then his eyes shift back to me and narrow. "Move."

"Let her go first."

"Sawyer, please. No. He will kill you," Jo cries.

I focus solely on her for a moment. "It's alright."

Jo shakes her head. "No." She fights against the biker's hold.

I take a slow step toward the Reaper's Nomads, and the president shoves Jo forward. "Walk," he orders with his gun aimed at the back of her head.

I see it in his eyes before he ever makes a move. The bastard has no intentions of trading my life for hers. His eyes stay on mine, and his lips curl into a sadistic smirk. I reach into my cut, producing my other gun, and aim in his direction. As the fucker stumbles backward, he fires.

Shots ring out around me. I watch Jo's body lurch forward.

"No!" I dash toward Jo, falling to my knees and catching her in my arms. "Jo, baby?"

"Sawyer," she moans, gripping at my cut. "Is Sawyer okay?"

"She's okay, baby." I hold Jo against me, shielding her from the chaos.

The gunfire exchange abruptly stops and things become quiet.

"I'm hit," I hear Wick announce.

A few feet away, I catch Riggs walking up to the Reaper's Nomads president, who's attempting to crawl away and reaching out for a weapon nearby. Riggs crushes the biker's hand beneath his boot before the bastard wraps his fingers around the grip of the gun. Without saying a word, Riggs aims his weapon and puts a bullet in the man's head.

Jo coughs. "I," she gasps, "can't breathe." She struggles for air as blood gurgles from her mouth. That's when I feel the warmth against my palm pressed against her back. I turn Jo's body slightly and notice her back, and my hand is soaked with blood.

"Shit," I hiss. "Prez!"

Riggs rushes toward me. "Fuck." he sees Jo struggling to breathe. "Get her to the car."

Cradling Jo's limp body, I lift her off the ground and carry her to my car. I climb into the backseat with her. Kiwi helps lower an injured Wick into the front passenger's seat, then jumps behind the wheel. "Go, go, go." I don't even take time to find out my brother Wick's injuries. I keep my eyes on Jo and turn her over when she coughs more blood. Kiwi speeds down the road, trying like hell to get us to the nearest hospital. Jo's breathing becomes more labored. "Hold on, baby." I grab hold of her hand, interlacing our fingers. I lean down and press my lips to hers. "You feel me, baby. Stay with me. I need you to hold on. Be strong for our daughter. She's waiting for you, baby." *God, don't you fuckin' take her. Not when I just got her back.*

Jo suddenly stops breathing. "Jo?" I give her a slight jostle. "Baby?" I press my fingers to the side of her neck, checking for a pulse. There isn't one. "No, goddamnit. No!" I slip Jo from my lap and lay her flat against the seat. "Kiwi, floor it. For fuck's sakes, make this car go faster," I plead as I start chest compressions.

I stop and check for a pulse again. "Fuck!"

I'm drowning in fear and desperation while trying to save the woman I love.

This is all my fault—my failure.

I check for a pulse again, and still nothing.

"Don't let go, Jo. Don't fuckin' let go."

EPILOGUE
FENDER

The sun is shining, casting a glow over the bayou, making it shine like there are millions of tiny diamonds floating on top of the water. Tilting my head back, I let the rays warm my face, and I can't help but think about all that I miss in this world. I've suffered a tremendous loss but am incredibly blessed for the family I do have. They've gotten me through some of my darkest days.

Having my family gathered out here at Pop's today, showing their love and support, proves just how lucky I am. There is no way I would have been able to make it through the past six months without them.

"Hey, Dad."

I look back over my shoulder to see Sawyer making her way down the dock toward me. "Hey, baby girl." I put my arm around my daughter when she sits down beside me on the edge of the pier.

"What are you doing out here by yourself?" she asks.

"Just thinkin'."

"Yeah." She leans her head against my shoulder.

We're both quiet for a minute before she whispers, "I miss her. I miss her so much."

"Me too, baby girl." I kiss the top of her head. "She may not be here with you physically, but she will always be with you in spirit."

Today is a big day for my girl. Sawyer is celebrating her sweet sixteen. Not having one of the most important women in her life here puts a bit of a gray cloud on the celebrations.

"You know she wouldn't have wanted you to be sad? She would have wanted you to smile, laugh, and have a wonderful time." I squeeze Sawyer closer to me.

"I know. And I am having a good time." Sawyer beams up at me. "Thanks for letting Jude come over."

"Yeah, yeah," I grumble, making Sawyer giggle. I have to admit the kid is pretty cool, and he treats Sawyer with respect. The boy even stuck by her side through her recovery after being shot. He doted on her. Even his family showed their support by coming by the house with ready-made meals, feeding us for a week. Turns out even his folks are cool, and they adore my daughter.

An ear-piercing whistle draws my and Sawyer's attention. When we look back toward the house, I see Kiwi motioning for us to come over. "Come on, baby girl." I climb to my feet, pulling Sawyer with me. "Time for cake."

When we walk into Pop's house, Maggie claps her hands. "There's the birthday girl. Come over here." Maggie ushers Sawyer over to the dining room table where the family is gathered around. Pop is standing at the head of the table. Beside him are Riggs, Luna, and their daughter. Then there are Wick and Tequila. I grin at the sight of Wick holding his sleeping baby daughter. Down the line are Nova, Promise, and their boy, along with Piper, Kiwi, Everest, Catcher. And, of course, June and Maggie. Lastly, there is Jude, Sawyer's boyfriend, along with her best friend, Maddy.

"Do you all really have to sing?" Sawyer hides her face in her hands as Maggie goes to light the candles on the cake.

"Yes, we do," Maggie laughs. "Now on three."

To my daughter's embarrassment, everyone sings happy birthday to her.

"Make a wish, baby girl."

Sawyer looks at me, then back at the cake. Closing her eyes, she blows out the candles.

"What did you wish for?" Jude asks.

"I can't tell you. Everyone knows if you say it out loud, it won't come true. "

"Well, I know one thing you wished for." I pull a set of keys from the front pocket of my jeans.

Sawyer screeches and starts jumping up and down. "Oh my God!"

"Sawyer, please tell me you didn't."

I grin down at Jo, who has her arms wrapped around my waist. She's giving me a look that says I'm in trouble.

"I might have." My grin gets bigger when Jo rolls her eyes.

Dangling the keys in the air, I look back at my daughter. "Happy Sweet Sixteen, baby girl."

"I can't believe this!" Sawyer charges me. "You're the best!" She swipes the keys from my hand and runs out of the house.

"In three, two, one," Jo counts down. A second later, we hear our daughter scream from the yard.

When we step outside, I see Sawyer in the front seat of the newly restored 1967 Shelby GT. And the look of pure joy on her face is worth the grueling hours spent making sure the car would be ready by today. It wasn't easy keeping it a secret. I kept the car out at Kiwi's place, where he helped me restore it.

"You spoil her."

I look down at Jo to see her watching our daughter with the biggest smile on her face.

"I know," I agree.

Jo tilts her head back and palms my cheek. "Thank you. Thank you for loving her the way you do and being the best father any girl could ask for."

As I gaze down upon my woman, there's a break in the clouds that allows a ray of sunlight to shine across her face, and at this moment, I can feel my mother's presence with us. This is what she wanted for me, Jo, and our daughter.

I was right earlier when I told Sawyer that her grandmother would always be with us. Right now, she's making her presence known.

Six months ago, I almost lost the love of my life, and my daughter almost lost her mom. I'm not saying Jo's road to recovery hasn't been challenging, because it has. Not only was Jo stabbed multiple times, but she was shot in the back—a sight that will forever be burned into my memory. Jo stopped breathing and her heart stopped beating before arriving at the hospital that day. I remember watching helplessly as the doctor shocked her several times in order to bring her back.

The weeks following were touch and go. Jo had surgery to repair the damage the bullet left behind and they brought in a plastic surgeon to stitch up the large gash she had across her chest.

Through it all, Jo's main focus was our daughter, who thankfully also made a complete recovery.

The strength my mother instilled in me and the bond I share with Jo helped get us through it all. If anything, the horrible ordeal taught us that together, we are stronger and can overcome anything.

Jo is nearly healed, and the three of us have spent every day of the past six months becoming the strong family unit we are today. We stopped fretting about the past and all our mistakes and starting looking toward our future together. We have decided to live in the here and now. I don't know what the future holds, but as long as I have the woman I love, our daughter, and my club, I'll be ready for whatever ride the universe wants to take me on.

Cupping Jo's face between the palms of my hands, I kiss her lips. "Thank you for loving me and giving me Sawyer; for giving me us."

"I love you, Sawyer."

"I love you too, baby."

Lightning Source UK Ltd.
Milton Keynes UK
UKHW021257110722
405684UK00007B/1340

9 798986 151601